2

WITHDRAWN

28

AND THEN YOU DIE

BOOKS BY JAMES E. MARTIN

THE FLIP SIDE OF LIFE

THE MERCY TRAP

THE 95 FILE

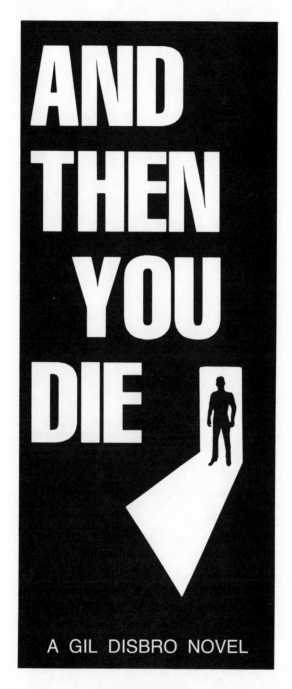

AND THEN YOU DIE

A GIL DISBRO NOVEL

James E. Martin

WILLIAM MORROW AND COMPANY, INC. • NEW YORK

Library of Congress Cataloging-in-Publication Data

Martin, James E., 1936–
    And then you die / James E. Martin.
        p.   cm.
    ISBN 0-688-11198-X
    I. Title.
    PS3563.A7243A83   1992
    813'.54—dc20   91-40661
                                                                                          CIP

Printed in the United States of America

First Edition

1 2 3 4 5 6 7 8 9 10

BOOK DESIGN BY LINEY LI

TO JENI,

WHO COULD ALWAYS

PULL THE WOOL

OVER MY EYES

AND
THEN
YOU
DIE

1

Everything I knew about my potential client came from an article in *Cleveland* magazine. Boyd Lassiter, a professor of economics at Baldwin-Wallace, had inherited the family business—a modest auto supply company dealing with Brook Park Ford and Lordstown General Motors. When a new federal emissions mandate went into effect, Lassiter discovered his company held the patent to a gasket that could make the catalytic converter 10 percent more effective. Suddenly, Lastec Inc. had the entire auto industry by the balls. Within six months, the big three domestic companies were kissing Lassiter's ass to get rights to the gasket, and the foreign manufacturers with U.S. sales were puckering up for their turn. Lassiter drove a hard bargain with all of them for the right to use the gasket and took his profits to Wall Street, where he used his academic theories to triple what he had already made. Ten months after the government's announcement, Lassiter was able to resign his teaching job to devote himself to a life of leisure while managing his investments. An American success story, thanks to some anonymous guideline writer in Washington.

One other thing I knew that hadn't been in the magazine article—he was in the market for the services of a private detective.

Following his success, Lassiter had moved into a Bratenahl manor house modestly known as Buckingham Estates. A private drive led to it from Lakeshore Boulevard through a quarter mile of parklike woods until I finally found the house itself, a massive Tudor mansion with its back windows overlooking Lake Erie. I drove up to it in my Chevrolet Caprice—which had no Lastec gasket, not even a catalytic converter—and passed through an arch into a courtyard bordered by the swimming pool, the three-car garage, and the main house. In the courtyard a man in a chauffeur's uniform was hosing down a bronze Mercedes with more attention to sanitation than the average operating room gets.

I parked as inconspicuously as I could and stepped out into a raw January morning. The courtyard was sheltered from the wind blowing off the lake, but it was still a long way from Miami Beach. Rivulets of water running off the sanitized Mercedes were already freezing on the blacktop of the courtyard. I walked toward the front door from my car with hands jammed in the pockets of my topcoat.

"Where do you think you're going?"

The words had come from the chauffeur who was shutting off his hose and placing his polishing cloth on the roof of the Mercedes.

"If you're not careful, those doors are going to freeze shut," I told him in a friendly tone.

"Think you can do a better job?" he asked, and started toward me. He was not all that tall, maybe five ten, but built with lots of specific gravity to every inch. As he drew closer, I saw the scar tissue around his eyebrows and the flattened knuckles of his big hands. He didn't look like a man I wanted to offend unnecessarily.

"Sorry. I didn't mean to get off on the wrong foot."

The chauffeur looked first at my car, which didn't have all the options, and then at me, who didn't either. "What do you want here?"

"I'm calling on Mr. Lassiter, if it's important for you to know that."

12

"It is." He drew himself upright and swelled his chest to show off his double-breasted gray uniform that would have hung well on Erich von Stroheim. "One of my duties is to keep undesirables away from Mr. Lassiter. He's been bothered by all sorts of salesmen since his money started multiplying."

"I'm not one of them. He called my secretary late yesterday afternoon and made an appointment for this morning." I started around him, but he did a sideway shuffle that put him in my path again.

"Not so fast. I need your name."

"Why? Did you lose your own?"

He had a face that had not been constructed for the display of humor. "Wisecracks I don't need. I'll ask this one more time: Your name?"

A straight answer seemed to be the quickest way of getting past him. "Gilbert Disbro." I took a step forward, and he laid a hand on my chest that could have covered the top of a poker table.

"Every Gilbert I ever knew was a cocksucking nance."

I looked down at his hand on my chest and then smiled when I looked up at him and winked. "I'm busy now, but maybe we can get together later this evening."

He stepped back as if touching me would contaminate him. "You still haven't told me your business."

"All right. I'm a casket salesman. I brought a midget model so you can bury the chimp."

"Huh?"

Sunset Boulevard," I explained. "They had faces then."

He shook his head in bewilderment. "You're whacko. You need some sense pounded into you."

"Do you think I could find someone to do it if I looked in the yellow pages?" By this time I had realized he was going to pick a fight with me no matter what I did.

"You don't have to look that far." He started swinging from his heels, a bad move for someone with his obvious experience. Having sized me up, he had decided that one good roundhouse would be half again what was needed to deal with me.

Before his fist had completed half of the scenic route, I uncorked two left jabs into his chops. They didn't hurt him that much. He blinked and shook his head, letting his fist go slack. He touched the back of his hand to his mouth and then looked at the blood on it. "You're too skinny for that to happen."

"It's the way my coat is tailored that fooled you."

He came at me again, throwing a punch I ducked. I feinted with a right and threw another left jab, taking advantage of my three inches in height on him to keep out of his reach. This time he was ready, taking a backward step that would have put him far enough away to drain the force from my punch. Instead of that happening, his foot landed on one of the rivulets of ice and skidded out from under him. He was on his way down, his jaw coming level with my waist, when I swung my right uppercut. His head snapped back, and the back of his skull rapped the blacktop driveway. Despite all that, he was not out. He rolled onto his side, tried to push himself up, and fell back.

"Take the nine count," I advised him, and went past him to the front door recessed in a Gothic arch. I had to ring the bell only once for a response.

The heavy oak door with iron straps, a prop from a Frankenstein movie, was opened by a Vietnamese man in a white houseboy's coat, soon enough to tell me my arrival had been anticipated. He smiled as if I had recently done him a favor, which might have meant he had been watching my thrilla with the chauffeur. "Yes?"

"Gilbert Disbro for Mr. Lassiter." I handed him one of my business cards.

He looked at it for what he thought would be long enough to have read it. He smiled at me some more. "Yes." He stepped back, opening the door wider so I could come in.

The door let me into a two-story hall with a Y-shaped staircase leading up to the second floor, someone's idea of the great hall in a Norman castle. The paneling, the woodwork, and the banisters on the staircase had all been done in dark, heavy wood, adding to the gloom of a winter day.

"Take coat?" the houseboy offered.

Considering the gloom of the place, I was tempted to leave it on. When I did surrender it, the houseboy handled it with the respect due a Burberry even though it was a standard London Fog. He draped it over his arm and gestured me toward a pair of sliding oak doors. He parted them and ushered me into the room beyond. I supposed it was the library because it had walls covered with bookshelves except for the space taken up by the fireplace and the windows. There was a desk somewhat smaller than a tennis court in front of a bay window looking out on to the courtyard and behind it a high-backed leather chair handed down by Oliver Wendell Holmes, Jr. Other chairs in the room were close relatives of it, scattered about so you could sit to read. It had the ambience of a men's club. What it didn't have was anyone using it.

"Where is Lassiter?" I asked the houseboy.

"Not here. Back soon." He bowed and backed through the sliding doors, pulling them shut from the hall side.

Which left me alone in the library, like a prisoner in a cell. I moseyed over to the desk and looked out the bay window in time to see the chauffeur pulling himself erect with the aid of the front fender of the Mercedes. After a bit, he picked up the hose and resumed his sterilization process. I wandered to the bookshelves to see what they held. The biggest section, not surprisingly, was works on economics by Ricardo, Marx, and Adam Smith—the originals and the twentieth-century aliases. Second in size was a section on American and European history since 1500, followed closely by biographies of figures in those periods. The rest was too miscellaneous to categorize, covering everything from a leather-bound set of Dickens to Robert Ludlum paperbacks. I picked up a *Portable Mark Twain* and settled into Oliver Jr.'s chair, where the light was good, to read through some of the shorter selections.

Time passes fast when Sam Clemens is amusing you, so I can't be sure how long I had been at it when tires screeched outside. I do know I had left only three cigarette butts in the ashtray, so it couldn't have been long. I looked up in time to see a black Porsche coming to a halt beside the Mercedes. The man who unfolded from it was too tall for such a small car, about six three. I recognized him from the photos that had accompanied the magazine article, seeing also that he was different in real life. Boyd Lassiter was forty-something, with a bean-pole physique that doesn't need a lot of exercise to hold itself together well into the middle years. His hair, at least the portion of it that showed below his sports car driver's tweed cap, was turning silvery gray about one hair in every five. The cap was an exact match for his soot-gray tweed topcoat, which in turn was an exact match for the legs of his soot-gray tweed suit. He was carrying an attaché case.

The chauffeur was waiting to report as soon as Lassiter emerged from the car. He listened while the chauffeur explained things to him and pointed to the icy patch. Lassiter stroked his chin while he received the news the way MacArthur reacted to the fall of Corregidor. When the chauffeur was done with his explanation, Lassiter turned his head to stare hard at him. Even though watching them for me was like seeing a silent movie, there was no mistaking the message in Lassiter's eyes: You failed me. The chauffeur dropped his chin onto his chest, and Lassiter strode toward his house.

After a few minutes of preliminary noises in the hall, the doors parted, and Lassiter strode into the library, stripped down to his three-piece suit but still carrying his attaché case. He stopped when he saw me sitting behind his desk with my ankles crossed on the corner. "Ah, Mr. Disbro, sorry you were kept waiting."

"Wasn't that part of your plan?" I asked.

He neither confirmed nor denied this but let a nucleus of a smile touch his lips. Up close, his features were reasonably handsome but not sculpted with smiling in mind. They belonged to a Puritan judge pronouncing sentence at a witch trial. "Gruznik says you're quick and surprisingly strong for one of your build."

I slapped Mark Twain shut and tossed the book onto Lassiter's desk, deliberately making noise doing it. "That stunt you just pulled was stupid and juvenile."

16

Lassiter tried doing a trick with his still-dark eyebrows that was supposed to show innocence. His face wasn't built to pull it off. "Stunt?"

"Putting your man up to picking a fight with me."

"You think Gruznik—"

"Worse than that," I went on without giving him a chance to finish his lie, "it betrays your opinion of me. I don't get a kick out of roughing somebody up. It's bad enough when I have to do it in the line of duty, let alone having to pass a test."

Lassiter considered and gave in too easily. "My apologies. Some very rough people are involved in this case. I wanted to be sure the man I employed was able to take care of himself." He smiled again at the finish of his backhanded compliment. "After all, you passed with flying colors."

I dropped my feet off the corner of his desk. "What is it I'm supposed to do?"

"In the fewest possible words, find my wife."

"Twenty dollars an hour, plus expenses," I said. "Five hundred dollars as a retainer."

He nodded. "Agreed."

"Fine." I stood up and brushed past him on my way to the door. "I quit."

2

"Wait! Please!"

The words came only after seconds of oppressive silence. I would have been halfway to my car except for the library door being stuck in its track. Instead of looking foolish struggling with it, I faced him again as if I were giving forgiveness serious consideration.

"Perhaps I have been gauche in my methods but you must understand I have no experience in these matters. I really am afraid of these men, and Gruznik can usually acquit himself admirably. I wouldn't want you to think too ill of me. Even if you can't work for me, at least let me give you some token of my sincerity. Let me at least pay you for your time."

The face I was looking at was not the face of the hardass who had dismissed Gruznik with a put-down glance. His gray eyes were softer, his eyebrows peaked over his nose, his eyelids pulled down at the outside corners.

"Besides, there is the personal factor," he went on. "Knowing you were a friend of Helen's, I wanted additional assurance I was not sending you into a situation you couldn't handle."

"You know Helen?" I asked.

"I'm barely acquainted with her, actually. We met at a conference about a year ago, when I was representing Baldwin-Wallace and she Cleveland State. I had heard about her divorce and—well—I was working toward making a pass. She let me know that her sex life was more than satisfactory. Later, through academic gossip, I heard she had a private detective living with her, hardly the usual for an associate professor of English. When I developed the need for such services, I naturally turned to you."

Don't weaken, I warned myself, and promptly weakened. "You said your wife is missing?"

"That was the shorthand version. It's actually much more complicated."

"As long as you're paying for my time, I might as well listen to your story. Maybe I can suggest someone."

"Excellent." Lassiter went behind his desk and put his attaché case down. He must also have touched some kind of buzzer, for within seconds the library doors parted to admit the Vietnamese houseboy. "What shall we have while we discuss this?" Lassiter wondered.

"Coffee," I said.

"Coffee, Tram." Lassiter held up two fingers. "For two."

Smiling and bobbing his head, Tram backed out of the library. I pulled up one of the extra chairs and dropped into it, reaching for a cigarette. Lassiter leaned back in the chair I had recently vacated and said, "A little over a month ago my wife left me. She went out to Reno to establish residency on a dude ranch and get a divorce."

"Do people still do that?"

"Renee would, if only for the excuse of gambling. It's one of her weaknesses." He sounded as if there were a long list to be enumerated at the proper time.

"Have you been in touch with her at all?"

"A few phone calls widely spaced. Our separation was not bitter. We should have done this years ago, but we stayed together out of habit more than anything else. When I hit it big, Renee realized any settlement would leave her fixed for life." He

19

brushed dirt from my heels off the corner of his desk. "The fact that I was once considering a dalliance with your mate tells as much about our marriage as anything."

I wondered. A simple question of fact had led to a discourse on his marital history. "You can't consider your wife missing simply because she's staying on a dude ranch in Nevada."

"True. Except that she is no longer on the Triangle K."

"If you're not in communication with her, how do you know that?"

"Otis T. Bremmel told me." Lassiter opened a desk drawer and removed a Rolodex holding business cards. He plucked one out and showed it to me.

CARAVAN HOTEL/CASINO

"A Division of Leisure Time Pursuits"

Otis T. Bremmel	Las Vegas
Finance Manager	Atlantic City

"Mr. Bremmel is in Cleveland this week, stopping over on his way to Atlantic City, staying at the Hanover House," Lassiter explained. "He looked me up yesterday, Monday, because he wanted to discuss the debt Renee has run up at the Caravan."

I looked at the card again but saw only the two cities listed. "That is in Vegas, not Reno."

He nodded to show me I had it right. "Renee has been running up a lot of debts on my credit cards."

"Gambling debts?"

"Purchases, mainly. Her gambling debts are separate. Bremmel told me they were giving her a line of credit up to a hundred thousand dollars at the tables, based on my rating. He also assured me they are comping her room. You understand that word—'comping'?"

I nodded. "Free room and board. It's like a loss leader at the discount store. They can afford to give it away because she's losing that much several times over each day at the tables."

"For someone with Renee's habits, it amounts to a form of kidnapping for ransom. Because she is getting free room and board, she doesn't want to leave, and as long as she stays at the Caravan, she continues to lose money to them. The ropes holding her may be velvet, but they are strong as log chains."

Tram returned bearing a silver tray with a coffee service. He set it down on an end table and provided a cup for me and for his boss. The business went smoothly because nothing required him to speak English. I waited until he was gone again. "So Bremmel was pressuring you to pay her gambling debts."

"He didn't put it in those terms. Considering our impending divorce, he wanted to know if I would honor more than the hundred thousand. I told him that Renee is welcome to gamble all she wants as long as she understands her losses will be subtracted from her settlement. It wouldn't displease me if she blows it all and ends up working there as a cocktail waitress to pay off her debt." His face showed the prospect of her degradation pleased him.

"Did Bremmel take it like a man when you told him that?"

"His only question was to wonder if the divorce settlement could be expected to stretch her line of credit to two hundred thousand. I assured him three times that would be very conservative, and he was happy. That ended our conversation, which was no worse than any serious talk with your banker. Except there was an air of menace in the room which wasn't improved by the associate he brought along. He looked like a gangster. Of course, many of those casinos in Las Vegas are connected to the mob, aren't they?"

"Sometimes." I stubbed out my cigarette. "Didn't you ever see *The Godfather*?"

"Of course I did. Memories of that are what worried me most. I decided to call Renee at the Caravan and warn her about the situation. Not that I expected her to heed me. If she used logic and reasoning at the crap table, she wouldn't have her problem with the odds—or any other problems. Anyway, I never got the chance. She had checked out."

"When was that?"

"Yesterday afternoon, our time, when I called. She wasn't in her room then, nor could the hotel operator locate her. That worried me enough to call your office."

"So soon? She hasn't been missing a day."

"Besides the fact that criminals are involved, Renee's behavior has been bizarre even by her standards. I'm still not used to being rich, but I'm learning that having money means people will scheme to take it from me. Renee could be my weak spot."

Somehow I felt more comfortable hearing his real worry was his pocketbook. He went on, "This morning I tried calling the Caravan again and learned she had checked out."

"She went back to the dude ranch?"

"No. But she had never checked out of there, either. Apparently, she simply left for the Caravan in Las Vegas without telling anyone where she was headed. There may have been a man involved."

"Is that a good guess, or do you have some reason for it?"

"Last night I also called Mrs. Kravitz, the owner of the Triangle K. She mentioned that she was having labor problems. A wrangler she called Harry had quit unexpectedly, and she was too shorthanded to worry about every guest. Knowing Renee, I drew the conclusion."

"Men and gambling. What other problems does she have?"

"Drugs. Alcohol. The one thing she doesn't do is smoke," he said pointedly as I set fire to another Camel.

"What kinds of drugs?"

"Angel dust, cocaine, grass. Two years ago, when I was a lowly teacher, she had to be hospitalized for a cure. It worked for a while but she went back, particularly on booze. That was her drug of choice when economics prevented her from finding something more potent. I've never known her to use heroin."

"It's the nineties," I said as if that would explain it all. "So what we know is that she's not in Reno and she's not in Vegas. That leaves a few points in the universe to be checked."

"My hunch is that she is still in Nevada," Lassiter told me in what he thought was private eye lingo. "This would be her fifth week for residency. Unless she has had a change of heart about the divorce, I can't understand her losing her residency status with only one week to go."

I was thinking that substance abusers are not always dependable when logical choices are involved. "How about her friends here in the Cleveland area? I'm looking for someone who might know what her plans are, someone she might have called or sent a postcard."

Lassiter permitted himself a laugh that was sired by more bitterness than humor. "If only you knew how useless that question is. Over the last few years, as her dependency has become worse, she has managed to alienate all our friends. Renee was an only child, and her parents have been dead for many years. I have often suspected that had some bearing on her preference for being alone. Alcohol and drugs were actually a wall she built up against the world to isolate herself."

He had been saying most of that with his eyes directed to the pen set on his desk. He raised them to me now. "The answer to your question is, she has no friends. The only person she might have said something to is Steve Stockman."

"What is his connection?"

"He was a musician Renee thought highly of. He had a band called the Laffer Curve that played in one of the clubs down in the Flats. Stockman? Laffer Curve? You see the pun?"

I nodded to assure him that my living with a college professor had raised my consciousness of national events.

"Renee was extremely enthusiastic about the band, dragging me down to hear them on weekends. Personally, I was bored with them—all noise and no melody you could hum. Apparently the public agreed with my judgment. I think the Laffer Curve dissolved. It didn't seem to bother Stockman. He lives quite well in one of those condominiums converted from an old warehouse down by the river." Lassiter must have seen a touch of skepticism on my face because he nodded and added, "Obviously he has a source of income besides his music. I suspect he deals in dope. More than suspicion. He was once arrested for sales."

"He's doing time now?"

"Nothing much ever came of it. It's one of the many episodes in Renee's past that have caused me so much pain." Regardless of the pain, he was waiting for the chance to tell me about it. I stayed silent and he added, "Renee was arrested for possession. I mentioned that she had been institutionalized. Well, that was a result of her arrest. The authorities let her commit herself voluntarily if she would name her supplier. She named Stockman, and the police set out to entrap him. They caught him making a sale, and he went to prison for a short time, but he's free now."

"You think Renee's still in touch with him? That Stockman doesn't hold a grudge?"

"When she got out of detox, she started using cocaine again within a matter of weeks. It had to come from somewhere."

"Do you know his exact address?"

"Afraid not."

Offhand I could think of only three ways of finding it. "Anyone else who might have been in touch with her?"

Lassiter's hesitation was not due to a failure of memory but to reluctance. "Audrey Carnahan." The name wriggled out of his mouth like a prisoner tunneling out of a cell. "She was a student of mine in economics class. After graduation, she went to work for Shearson and then, when I came into my sudden wealth, I financed her in setting up a business of her own, North Coast Investments in the Arcade. We have been working closely together in Wall Street ventures."

"How does she connect with your wife?"

"Audrey had to take a trip to San Francisco two weeks ago. On her way back, she stopped off in Reno to see Renee, partly at my behest. Audrey reported to me what Renee was doing but—well—I think she may have been holding back, either to spare my feelings or because Renee swore her to secrecy. Perhaps, under the circumstances, she would tell you about it."

"A phone call from you might help pave the way for me so I don't spend a lot of time in the waiting room."

Lassiter rubbed his chin as if he were looking for a spot his razor had missed. "Am I hearing you right? Are you agreeing to take this case after all?"

"As long as we have an understanding," I said. "I can follow up on the leads you've given me here in Cleveland. Whatever they tell me, there's a good chance some additional work is going to have to be done in Nevada. If that comes to pass, there are two ways we can handle it. I can farm it out to an agency out there, or I can go myself. If you send me, there will be expenses involved—plane tickets, hotel room, car rental, and at least two thousand cash in advance in case I have to spend something at the tables."

"Agreed," he said without hesitation. "Are you sure the two thousand will be enough?"

"I'm counting on winning and building it into real money." I got out one of my standard contract forms, filled in the necessary blanks, and passed it to him for his signature, which upgraded me to the working class.

"Anything else?" he asked.

"A good description of your wife and a recent photo."

The description came hard for him. I had to pry it out with a long series of questions. Renee, now thirty-six years old, five feet six, 120 pounds, auburn hair, and green eyes. No tattoos. No scars. Finding the photo was almost as hard. He had none sitting out and had to search his drawers to find what he had done with them. The one he gave me was a posed studio shot with a ghostly profile hovering over her shoulder. Her hair was worn shoulder length with lots of curls, going half wild. Her face, which showed every one of her years, had the embalmed look of a corpse.

"It's not a very good likeness," Lassiter commented.

"What's wrong with it?"

He took the photo back from me and studied it. "Vitality missing, I guess. She is so manic, so wired, that any still photo is going to seem incomplete. Also, she recently had surgery repairing her nose—the effects of snorting cocaine—while she was hospitalized. The result is that her nose appears thinner now when you look at her face-on. In profile, that slight curve is less pronounced."

When I had studied it enough to decide that even with the

changes she would be worth hitting on in a singles bar, Lassiter removed the photo from its frame and gave it to me. "It's yours to keep. I have others."

I put it away with his contract and drained what remained in my coffee cup. "Provided I see everyone today, I should have something to report tomorrow."

"Take your time and be thorough," he advised, and then gave me his unlisted phone number in case I needed to reach him quickly. As he guided me to the door, he asked a final question: "Do you mind telling me why you changed your mind and went to work for me after all?"

"Your money and your conspicuous consumption. I decided some of it should find its way to my pocket."

He enjoyed that. "A check for your fees and expenses, including your Las Vegas contingency fund, will go out today."

Tram was waiting in the great hall with my topcoat. While he was showing me out, I thought of the incomplete answer I had just given Lassiter, true enough as far as it went but dropping short of the whole truth. His situation had plucked a chord in me because I could empathize with his feelings. When Linda had left me, I had known the ambiguous emotions of an abandoned husband, the swings from "good riddance" to a nagging sense of responsibility compounded by the suspicion that if only I had loved her better, maybe I wouldn't have driven her away. Typical of that guilt trip, I was already wondering what Lassiter had done to turn his wife into a junkie.

In the courtyard, Gruznik had finished the sterilization of the Mercedes and now was working on the Porsche, even though it had probably been used for no more than an hour this morning. He had not touched my Caprice. I stopped and watched him.

"It was the ice," I told him. "If you hadn't slipped, I never would have had a shot at you."

Gruznik took his eyes off the Porsche and let me have a view of his scar tissue. "You tell him that?"

"Yeah."

"Asshole won't listen. He's probably going to fire me over it."

"You were looking for a job when you got this one."

"Maybe I can promote a couple fights to tide me over. That's all I was doing with this job anyway, filling in between bouts."

"Been working here long?"

"Since October. It's a soft berth, really, and it provides me a nice place to live over the garage. If he don't fire me, I'll probably stick with it awhile longer. See me through the winter."

I nodded my approval of his plans for his life and returned to my car. The windows had frosted in the short time I had been inside. I started the motor, waiting for the defrosters to work. When I had clear vision, I headed for the Shoreway downtown to start earning my fee.

3

A block east of the pink BP America Building on Superior sits the soot-blackened stone Hanover House. I backed into a parking space on Short Vincent and entered the Hanover by its side entrance. The desk clerk parted with Otis T. Bremmel's room number as if she were giving away nuclear secrets and directed me to a house phone. I called upstairs and got an asthmatic voice saying, "Bremmel."

"Disbro."

There was a pause while he waited for me to add something. Finally he said, "I don't recognize that name."

"No reason why you should. I represent Boyd Lassiter. There are some questions he neglected to ask in yesterday's conversation concerning his wife."

Another pause while he ran that over in his mind. If I knew about his meeting with Lassiter, I must be what I claimed. He said, "And you would like to ask them now? Very well, come on up. I can spare you some time."

It was far less hassle than I had been prepared to face. Minutes later I was stepping off the elevator on Bremmel's floor and knocking on his door. When it opened I was on eye level with a

28

necktie—a shoestring tie held in place by a silver and turquoise slide. Somewhere above the tie was a face, but I couldn't see it until I leaned back for a perspective. It was a dark face that was all planes and angles, weathered and leathery, showing his Indian heritage. And it was elevated well above mine, helped only a little by his cowboy boots. Barefoot he still would have been six four or five. He could well have been the man who frightened Lassiter. He was doing a good job of intimidating me.

"You're from Lassiter?" he asked.

I showed him one of my cards. He looked at it and turned his head into the room. Besides the cowboy boots and the string tie, he wore a shirt with yokes across the shoulders and a pair of tan Western-cut pants with tunnel belt loops and horizontal pockets. His belt was wide, carved, and held by a square buckle that advertised Winchester. "It's that Disbro character."

"Show him in, Clint." That was the same asthmatic voice that had spoken to me on the house phone.

Clint jerked his head and led the way. Following him, I saw that his belt supported a holster behind his right hipbone holding a single-action hogleg with a plow-handle grip. At first I thought it was an old Colt, but then I saw the target sights and realized it was a Ruger Blackhawk, the twentieth-century copy of the old Peacemaker. I shut the door behind me while Clint transported my card to the other man in the room.

He sat in one of the chairs with a room service table set before him holding the remains of breakfast. Sitting, he was a squat man of fifty, going bald frontally and wearing rimless round glasses with thick lenses. Even so, he had to hold my card three inches from his nose. "Private detective?"

"I do work for Lassiter from time to time."

He laid my card aside and stood up to stretch his hand out to me across the table. Standing, he was still short and squat, wearing a silk robe over his white shirt and suit trousers. "I am Otis T. Bremmel, of course. My associate is Clint Pettibone. The two of you should have much in common. He is on the security staff of the Caravan in Las Vegas."

I shook hands with Bremmel but Clint stayed out of reach. Somehow I had trouble imagining us cozying up to one another.

Bremmel was showing what a good host he could be. "Sit down, Mr. Disbro. Please have some breakfast. There is plenty left. At least a cup of coffee?"

I accepted the coffee, which Bremmel poured from a silver pot into an unused cup. Clint sat on the foot of the bed to look at the television screen showing an old Randolph Scott Western.

"What facts did we forget to pass on to Mr. Lassiter?" Bremmel inquired.

"Details. He's still concerned for his wife's welfare even if the divorce is pending."

"Living in Nevada, I probably see more than my share of divorcées," Bremmel noted. "It's not at all unusual to see husbands looking out for the ex-wife's welfare long after the final decree."

"Then what is the real story on Renee Lassiter?"

"She simply checked into the Caravan and proceeded to spend plastic money and gamble."

"Alone?"

A tiny smile touched Bremmel's pouty lips and then was gone, like a groundhog peeping out of his hole. He thought he understood what was really bothering Lassiter. "Clint, bring me that folder." He reached inside his robe and brought out a cigar. "Do you mind?"

"Not at all."

"These days you have to be careful around so many people."

"Let them wear gas masks. I spent all those years being polite and asking permission to smoke. Now they want to pass laws to prevent me from doing it. Piss on nonsmokers."

Clint had gone away from Randy Scott, who had roped a wild horse and was struggling to settle it down, and picked up an attaché case in the corner. He took a file folder out of it and brought it to Bremmel.

"Once Mrs. Lassiter checked in—alone—she came to me to open a line of credit. Naturally, news of her husband's recent dealings on Wall Street had reached us, so I had no hesitation about extending credit to her." Bremmel took the folder from Clint and went through it to find what he wanted—a manila envelope large enough to hold a stack of five-by-seven photos. He passed one of them to me.

It was a photo of Renee at a crap table taken by a surveillance camera. I recognized her with some difficulty, for Lassiter had been right when he told me her nose surgery had altered her appearance. But it was more than what the plastic surgeon had done to her that was responsible for the change. She had been caught holding her right fist by her ear, which I interpreted to mean she was holding a pair of dice, about to cast them. In the act, her eyes had come alive and were burning with an intensity usually associated with malarial fever. Her lips were parted to show her white teeth in a grin that had little to do with pleasure or satisfaction but the intensity of someone performing a task with dedication. She was wearing a cocktail dress with narrow straps across the shoulders, low-cut to display cleavage as she leaned forward.

When I looked up I found Bremmel watching me while he stripped the cellophane off his cigar. "See anything unusual?"

"No," I confessed.

He brought out more photographs and dealt them out face-up like a hand of showdown poker. They were all variations of the same pose, taken on different days because Renee wore different dresses. Sometimes she was at a roulette table, other times blackjack. Always there was a drink at her elbow.

"What are you trying to prove? That the lady gambles?"

Bremmel lit his cigar with a gold butane lighter and used the butt end for a pointer at the first photo he had showed me. "See that man?"

He was in the crowd around the crap table, a well-built guy of thirty with a dark Tom Selleck mustache and the features of a leading man. He wore a Western-style shirt and a straw Stetson on the back of his head, letting a lock of dark hair fall over his forehead.

I shook my head.

"Now look here." Bremmel moved the end of his cigar to a

photo taken at the roulette wheel. Same guy, except this time he wore no hat and a Hawaiian shirt, letting his unruly hair go wild. "And here." Bremmel now pointed to one of the photos at the blackjack table. Same guy again. This time he wore a sports jacket over a polo shirt without a tie and his hair was greased back.

Bremmel let me look over the rest of the pictures for myself and find the same man in each one. Each time he had altered his appearance in subtle ways. A business suit and horn-rimmed glasses. A T-shirt with a Budweiser label and a Dodgers baseball cap. But he was always there, across the table or around the corner from her.

"Are they together?"

"We can't establish that." Bremmel gathered up the pictures and put them away. "We had him followed when he left the casino. He goes to a cheap motel while she goes up to her room. They have no contact with one another, except at the gaming tables where they act like strangers. Yet they come as a set."

I picked a piece of bacon off his plate and nibbled it. "So what if they are together?"

"The man's name," Bremmel said as if it were supposed to mean something, "is Harry Winch. At least that's the one he uses more often than any other. He used to work at the Caravan, as a dealer, a couple years ago. He quit and did some other things. Sold used cars. Speculated in real estate developments around Tahoe. Then we lost track of him."

"Why did he quit?" It seemed to be the question Bremmel was waiting for me to ask.

"He was cheating us."

"I thought you had a tight security system."

"We do, but he wasn't pocketing chips. He was working with a partner. Several partners. When they sat in the game, Winch let them win. No cheating with shaved cards or any such thing. He was more subtle. A few dumb bets and the house loses a hand when it should have won. Nothing too big, nothing too gaudy. Later he meets his partner and splits the winnings. It could have gone on for a long time. The worst thing we could get him for was being a bad dealer, but he quit before that came up."

"So now you think he's gone back to a partnership, with Renee Lassiter this time."

Bremmel puffed his cigar and took his time before he nodded. "He always plays where she plays. He always bets against her. She's rolling for her point, he bets she'll crap out. She plays black on the roulette wheel, he bets red. Like that. She loses more than she wins. He wins more than he loses. In the last week, he's taken us for fifty thou."

"And she's dropped what? Two hundred grand?" I pointed out. "You're still way ahead and they're way behind, even if they are working in tandem. Maybe he's just being smart. He's pegged her for a loser, so he's betting with the house. Is there a law against that?"

"We don't like smartass players working a scam on us."

"What scam?" Wondering why I was feeling compelled to defend Renee and her boyfriend, I reached for a cigarette to help my thinking processes. "I'm not up on the subtleties of gambling, but I can't see where they could be coming out ahead when they're handing you three dollars for every one they take out."

Bremmel got up from his chair, jammed his cigar in his teeth, and strolled over to his window which looked out on to Superior. He stood there rocking slightly on his heels. On the TV screen, Randolph Scott was figuring finally that Douglass Dumbrille was secretly head of the outlaw band, as Gabby Hayes had been saying all along.

"This town is coming back," Bremmel judged by what his window showed him. "You went through some bad times under Dennis Kucinich, but you're rebounding now. I was raised here, you know." He glanced my way to make sure I heard that. "Out there on the East Side, on Cedar before the blacks took over. I started out doing favors for Shondor Birns, God rest his soul. Spent a lot of time right around the corner of Short Vincent. That's where I met Bill Veeck when he owned the Indians. Of course, I was just a snot-nosed kid then. When I was a little older, Shondor let me work for him, running numbers. He gave me money to go to accounting school because I was good with figures and because my eyes weren't so hot for street work. He introduced me to Moe Dalitz, who put me in touch with people in Vegas, which got me where I am. The last time I ever cried was when I heard about Shondor's car blowing up and him with it."

I visualized the civic people erecting a statue to Shondor Birns on Public Square next to Tom Johnson.

"Suppose," Bremmel said, suddenly jumping twenty years to the present, "that Mrs. Lassiter doesn't think of it as her money. It's her husband's money and she's divorcing him, so why not lose it to make a little more she can keep?"

"If Winch is her boyfriend," I countered, "and she wants him to have fifty thousand, why not just give it to him?"

"She might figure this way it's covered up. And she gets the thrill of gambling. That would be important to her."

"She has to know that whatever she loses is going to come out of her settlement eventually. Meanwhile, you're still ahead on a three-to-one ratio."

Bremmel gnawed at the problem the way he gnawed his cigar butt. "Then maybe it's an investment. Maybe there's something coming we don't see, the big kill."

"Not very likely. She checked out of the Caravan yesterday."

The news failed to surprise him the way I thought it would. "I know. I talked to headquarters this morning."

"Then she's out of your hair."

"And in yours. She also booked a flight back here last night. What are the details, Clint?"

Clint took his eyes off the television long enough to look at a notepad by the telephone. "Leaves Las Vegas this afternoon. Arrives Cleveland eight-twenty local time."

My shocker had fizzled but Bremmel's had worked on me. "What brings her back?"

"Who knows? Maybe she wants to kiss and make up with her husband." Behind Bremmel's thick-lensed glasses, something was going on that I didn't understand. I knew he was watching me for my reaction.

I put out my cigarette and finished my coffee. "It appears I'm wasting your time. I'd better warn Lassiter his wife is coming home."

Bremmel put up no struggle to keep me there as I made my exit. In the lobby, I had every chance to go to a pay phone to call Lassiter, but I passed them up without bothering to analyze why. During my conversation upstairs, I had sensed vibrations pitched just outside the range of human hearing. Otis T. Bremmel had cause for concern beyond what he had told me. I figured I had better gather as much information as possible before I acted on anything. I owed that much value to my client for his money.

4 Geography dictated my next stop. The Arcade, where North Coast Investments had its offices, sits just west on Superior across East Sixth Street from the Hollenden House. Short as the walk was, it seemed longer with the wind slicing through my clothes. I was grateful when I came to the grimy Gothic arch leading into the building.

The Arcade dates from 1890, long before Hyatt started building hotels with a massive atrium, but the principle was known even then. Five stories high under a golden skylight, the Arcade's central gallery is dominated by a massive Romanesque staircase that has been used for staging everything from grand opera to weddings. The lobby floor is a mini shopping mall surrounded by all kinds of stores and restaurants, even a Waldenbooks. The upper floors have balconies surrounding the gallery with more restaurants and shops on the second floor. The third level is supposed to be the start of offices but the building's owners have had trouble filling them. Rents, as a result, are a bargain compared to most downtown space.

The ideal time to see the Arcade is the lunch hour when office workers from all over downtown flock into it to watch the passing parade of humanity while they eat, preferably at a side-walk café or in a window seat in one of the restaurants. The earliest arrivals were already claiming their choice seats as I climbed the central stairs. Everything you would ever want to know about Cleveland—or any other city—can be seen here as if a sociologist had built it as a scale model for demonstration purposes. Bag ladies, attorneys, pimps, secretaries, workers, pensioners—all rub shoulders here whether they are frequenting the boutiques or simply cutting through to get out of the cold on Euclid Avenue.

North Coast Investments was on the fourth level, where car-penters were still working to divide the space into smaller of-fices. I held the door for a pair maneuvering a sheet of drywall through the double glass doors while somewhere inside a power drill shrieked with a noise appropriate to a dentist's office. I fol-lowed the carpenters only as far as the reception desk. Behind it sat a Joe College type in a sleeveless argyle sweater.

"May I help you?" he asked.

My first instinct was that he must be someone filling in for a few minutes while the receptionist went to the can. Then my sexist thinking faded as I realized he was the receptionist. His eyes dared me to make something of it, but I had already had my prelunch brawl that day. "I'm supposed to ask for Audrey Carnahan."

"Is Ms. Carnahan expecting you?"

"Boyd Lassiter was supposed to have set up a quick appoint-ment for me." I showed him one of my cards.

He consulted an appointment book open on his desk. There was a lot of blank space on the pages. "I don't see any time for a Mr. Disbro."

"Tell you what, Jack. Why don't you buzz Ms. Carnahan and see what she has to say about it. Maybe it was too important to go through you."

He bristled at that for some odd reason. "Ms. Carnahan's time is valuable."

"Look at me," I said, "and visualize Boyd Lassiter is standing here. Treat me the way you'd treat him, and you'll be all right. They might let you hold the hose the next time they water the stock."

He glared at me in a way not calculated to encourage familiarity and then reluctantly reached for the phone when I didn't melt. He spoke on the phone briefly and hung up as if it had brought him bad news. "Ms. Carnahan's office is at the end of the hall."

I smiled. "See? Charm works every time." I took off my topcoat and tossed it onto his lap. "Hang that up, would you?"

The hall down which I was being sent had been created by the panels of gray drywall now smeared with splashes of plaster. A doorway led into the room where all the construction noises were coming from. I glanced inside to see what shape it was taking. High on one wall, just below the suspended ceiling, was a rectangular panel across which ran stock quotations in green electronic computerspeak. When finished, the room would have chairs like a theater facing the screen. Rooms like that make me think of horse parlors.

My destination was the door at the end of the hall, which opened as I approached. The woman standing there was not very tall and tried to compensate for it with platform shoes and an outfit in charcoal-gray with a white pinstripe. Her hair was cut short, long enough to cover her ears but not to touch her shoulders. She had a round face that was attractive enough, but men had always told her she was cute and she resented it and adjusted her life to compensate for it so men would say she was competent.

"I'm Audrey Carnahan," she announced as I drew near.

We shook hands and she brought me into her spacious office where one wall was a plate glass window looking out on to the gallery. There were heavy curtains that could be drawn across it for privacy. Her desk was kidney-shaped with a credenza behind it and a computer terminal on one side so that her work area was a kind of three-sided corral.

"So Boyd hired a private detective." She regarded me the way she would have examined a blouse displayed on a department store mannequin. "At least you're presentable. My experience with private detectives hasn't been edifying. I thought they were all smarmy balding men who peep through motel registers."

"Who's your experience been with?"

"Fox Fax."

"Sleaze, Incorporated," I agreed. Gus Fox ran a one-man operation that specialized in flagrante delecto photography.

Audrey picked up a small watering can with a long spout. "My ex-husband had him following me at the time of our divorce." She turned away from me and carried the watering can over to a plant hanging from a chain. There were all kinds of plants in the room, sitting in pots or hanging wherever there was space. Green leaves and hanging vines were the best I could make of them. None seemed to bear flowers. If I had seen any of them growing in a yard, I would probably have chopped them down with the lawn mower.

I said, "Liberalized divorce laws should have put men like Fox out of business, but they keep hanging on. That's not my bag anyway."

She finished watering the plant, set the long-spouted can down, and entered her work corral. She settled into her chair, which had been jacked up for additional height so that she seemed taller sitting down. I would have bet her feet weren't touching the floor. "What does Boyd want from you?"

"There are some strange circumstances about the way Renee is living in Nevada. Lassiter wanted me to check with you because you're one of the few people from this area who have seen her."

Audrey plucked a cigarette from the pack lying on her desk and tapped it in a gesture she had learned from Joan Crawford. "I spent a few hours with her one afternoon. That hardly qualifies me as an expert on her life-style."

"Lassiter thought she might have said something you didn't tell him."

Audrey lit her cigarette and blew smoke over her shoulder. "Anything I know I've already told Boyd."

"There's nothing you would want to hold out?"

"Obviously, Renee was not about to describe her sex life in clinical detail, if that's what you're fishing for. What has she done, anyway?"

"Gambling. Losing heavily. Lassiter has the notion she's being held a semiprisoner in a Las Vegas club while they bleed her dry in the casino."

Audrey inhaled another puff while she considered it. "Possible. You said Las Vegas? Not Reno?"

"Did she say anything to you about intending to move from the dude ranch?"

"She seemed content on the Triangle K. If she wanted to gamble, it was only a short drive to Sparks, which is next to Reno. She wouldn't have any trouble getting a bet down there."

"Lassiter didn't tell me anything about your visit with her. He was counting on you filling me in. Why don't you just tell me about it? You never know when a small detail might be important."

Audrey glanced at the watch on her wrist as if calculating how much time she could spare. It seemed to me the only people working in this office were the carpenters.

"You knew I'd been on a business trip to San Francisco? That I arranged a layover in Reno on the return flight?"

"When was that?"

"The first week of the new year. Two weeks ago now. The whole layover lasted only five hours until I had to fly to Denver and make connections east. Renee met me at the airport and drove me out to the Triangle K, which is in the wilds toward Pyramid Lake."

"She has a car out there?"

"She borrowed it from another one of the guests, a woman also putting in her time for a divorce. It was a dilapidated red Rabbit." She added that last in irritation at having her narrative interrupted. "She spent some time showing me around, and then we sat in the lounge and talked, and then it was time for me to go back."

"What did you learn?"

"The biggest news? There's a difference between cowboys and wranglers. Did you know that?"

"Cowboys herd cattle. Wranglers handle horses." She seemed surprised that I would know that, so I asked, "Do they all look like Ben Johnson?"

"More like Paul Fix, old and leathery and arthritic. Except for one. He was the house gigolo, lots younger and better looking, the kind who would slip in a cheap feel while helping a woman into the saddle. We were barely introduced when he started coming on to me."

"And maybe to Renee?"

Audrey stubbed out her cigarette in the ashtray. "Not in my presence, but knowing Harry's character, I couldn't imagine him making an exception."

"Had Renee been drinking?"

"I've never known her to be out of reach of a glass. She drank while we were sitting in the lounge."

I ran a finger over my mustache and spread out all I knew about Audrey Carnahan. She called Lassiter by his first name, pronouncing it as if she were referring to the pope. Her own divorce had involved a bedroom peeper. She had been closely associated with Lassiter as his student while she was still married. She did not like Renee. I tried to imagine the worst possible outcome from her perspective. "Weren't you even a little surprised when Renee talked about coming back to Cleveland to patch things up?"

I could have reached across the desk and slapped her and got less of a reaction. Her mouth opened as if she wanted to curse me. Then it closed. Then she reached for another cigarette and began the Joan Crawford tap. "It was only a fleeting thought. She changed her mind fifty times."

"Fifty-one," I corrected. "She has a ticket for a plane that will be landing at Hopkins this evening."

The cigarette broke in her fingers. "Goddamn it!" She might have been directing that at the loose tobacco on her blotter but I didn't think so. "Does Boyd know?"

"I haven't had a chance to tell him yet. I only learned about it a few minutes ago."

"She's up to something." Audrey took out another cigarette and lit it quickly before she could shred it. "She's figured that it would be worth more for her to go on being Mrs. Lassiter for a while longer."

"Does that upset your plans?" I asked.

She had been scooping the remains of the broken cigarette into her wastebasket. She looked up at me with menace. "Meaning?"

"With Lassiter divorced, he would be fair game for you. If Renee gets back in the picture, your chances go down the tubes."

"I don't like your insinuations that something is going on between Boyd and me!" She stood up to impress me but she was too short to make it effective.

"I'm not making judgments," I told her quickly. "I would be the last person in line of that. All I'm asking is complete honesty in your answers. That way we can both help him."

Corny as the appeal was, it served to calm her. She inhaled deeply and folded her arms across her breasts. "When I was in college, I was one of Boyd's students. He was my favorite teacher, so naturally I worked hard for him. He appreciated my efforts, and I received top marks. When I graduated, he wrote me very good recommendations. When I was selling stocks, we saw each other from time to time and generally kept in touch. When my marriage started falling apart, he was there to support me. Now that he has come into a fortune, he's set me up in this business, which is a good investment for him. My efforts have helped him double what he started with. Nothing beyond that has to be explained."

"Uh-huh. And all Gus Fox could have collected on you two was photos of you adding debits and credits."

"Gus Fox followed us and took many photos of us getting in and out of cars, eating meals together, entering a hotel where we went to the conference room for a business meeting, and other innocent things like that. Nothing evil was in any one photo, but the cumulative effect could have been interpreted to mean something else. I settled my divorce claims for far less than I had coming to me to avoid bad publicity."

"Maybe. Now are you going to tell me you have no interest in Lassiter?"

"He is one of the most attractive men I've ever met. A year or two down the road when he's free, I might allow myself to think about it—provided the Prince of Wales hasn't proposed by that time."

She had spunk; I gave her that. Because she did, I was inclined to go along. "Still, you're not that fond of Renee."

She looked down to flick ashes into her ashtray. "That's no secret. In my opinion she's spoiled, self-indulgent, and self-destructive. Her whole life is a case of suicide by gradual degrees. She has been nothing to Boyd but an albatross around his neck. As long as she lives, Boyd's life will be held back."

"You sound like you're afraid he'll take her back."

"He might. Boyd has always been ambivalent in his passions toward her. Desire and hatred so mixed he never knows whether to kiss her or strangle her." She took a final drag and crushed her cigarette out. "If you don't mind, I do have other appointments."

The hint came when I had learned as much as my gray cells could deal with at this point. I said good-bye and walked down the corridor-in-the-making and took my topcoat down from its rack. The male receptionist was watching as if he had never seen it done before.

"You could do the same thing," I told him. "Put on your coat and walk out."

"I'm satisfied where I am," he answered.

"Sure you are. You're bubbling over with joy." I waved farewell and walked out the door.

5

When I left North Coast Investments, I faced a moral dilemma: I was almost exactly halfway between my office and home. The only duty I had left was making a call to Lassiter to inform him of his wife's imminent arrival. The home phone and the office phone worked equally well. At last I decided it was too early in the afternoon to call it a day. I started my car, steering it in the general direction of my office.

Before I could get there, I remembered I was forgetting to eat lunch again. That's no crime on most days, but now I had an expense account. Let Lassiter treat me. I stopped at a restaurant on Old River Road where it curves and lingered over a meal the way you can do when you have no pressing business later. Finished, I drove uphill to West Third Street.

Behind the Justice Center is a line of buildings slated for demolition and overdue by two decades. On the ground floor of one of them are a pawnshop and a used furniture store with a flight of stairs between them leading up to the second-floor offices. After I had parked in the reserved lot behind the building, I climbed that flight of stairs to the pebbled glass door at the top lettered:

MOE GLICKMAN
BAIL BONDS

Gilbert Disbro

Investigations

I pushed through the door into the tiny lobby that allows two steps between the door and the counter. A wire mesh screen fills the space between the counter and the ceiling as if it were guarding the national debt. At her desk behind the screen sat pudgy Gladys Keego and beside Gladys was Rolf, her attack-trained German shepherd. One of them barked at me when I came in.

"There you are," said the other one, Gladys. "How's the big case going?"

"Nearly wound up."

"You going to be free tomorrow morning? Wally wants to know on account of he has a bail jumper to be picked up."

When I had been laid off by the Cleveland Police Department, I had scrounged around for work. Moe Glickman had given me a few jobs bounty hunting for his bail jumpers. I thought I was doing temporary work until I would be called back as soon as the politicians straightened out the budget. As it turned out, they never did. When I saw my chances fading, I applied for my P.I. ticket and had to list an office address. Moe let me fix up a spare room here that would pass muster. He charged me ridiculously low rent on the condition I would help out Wally Stamm, his full-time man. The arrangement suited me because the reward money helped tide me over slack periods when clients didn't call. So far I was avoiding food stamps.

"I should be free," I told Gladys. "Let me make a phone call and find out for sure."

I walked past the bench where this afternoon's collection of losers sat waiting, clutching titles to cars or deeds to homes or savings account books they could put up as collateral to spring a relative or friend from jail. They put up 10 percent of the bail amount (which Moe kept) and got the surety to turn over to the jailer across the street. The suspect then was allowed to go free until the date of trial. If he failed to show, Moe was stuck with paying the full amount to the court. Not liking to do that, he would send Wally Stamm or me to track down the suspect. If we dragged him back in, Moe was saved the forfeit and showed his appreciation with a reward. As agents of a bondsman, Wally and I were authorized to carry guns and pursue the suspect wherever we needed to go, without worrying about technicalities like extradition.

Beyond the waiting bench, a short hall led to my office, outside the caged area to show I had nothing valuable to protect. It was cramped quarters made even more cramped by a ceiling that slanted down. That was all right. I seldom had to impress anyone. I settled into my swivel chair and dialed Lassiter's unlisted number.

"What have you learned?" he asked when we had completed the preliminaries.

"Renee will be home tonight. She's on a flight that lands at Hopkins at eight-twenty."

Silence. I shook out a cigarette and lit it. Finally Lassiter said, "You're sure?"

"Bremmel told me. He had called Vegas and found out she booked the flight through the Caravan."

"She never told me she was coming. What is she up to?"

"Maybe she's coming to see someone else," I offered. "Maybe she intends to turn around and go back."

"Well, you stay with it. Meet her plane when she comes in. Follow her and see where she goes."

"She might lead me right to your place."

"I'll be waiting," he promised.

We talked a little longer about business matters, during which he assured me my check was in the mail. When we had hung up, I went back down the hall to let Gladys buzz me through the door into the caged area of the office. Wally Stamm had come in while I had been on the phone. He was sitting at his desk now, a big black man with menace exuding from him strong enough to make him every Klansman's nightmare. He had his coat off, wearing a turtleneck sweater that exposed his two stainless steel magnums in twin shoulder holsters.

"Hear you've been out cavorting with rich white folks up at the big manor house," he greeted me.

"Quite a sight. They keep pickaninnies on leashes for pets and have an overseer riding through the grounds with a black-snake whip over his saddle horn."

Wally shrugged. "Their money's good. Have you earned enough of it for one day?"

"There's no such thing as enough, but Gladys tells me you have an errand tomorrow."

"Henry Justice Goodfellow." He skimmed a reward dodger to my side of the desk. It showed a black man with a goatee whose offense had been armed robbery and assault. "He has a girlfriend on Kinsman. When he went down south to hide out, she let another boyfriend move in with her. This morning she booted out the boyfriend for a few days, so it looks like Mr. Goodfellow is coming back. The boyfriend thinks we would be doing him a favor if we picked up Goodfellow. Then the boyfriend could move in permanently."

"How do we handle it?"

"Hit the place early tomorrow and scarf him up while he's still in bed."

I nodded. "Looks like I can take the time for that."

So our deal was made. I went back to my office and typed up a progress report on the work I had done for Lassiter that day. By three o'clock I was ready to treat myself to a few hours' rest before I met a plane.

The house where I was living then was in Ohio City, originally the other community on the west bank of the Cuyahoga. Although the town was absorbed by Cleveland long before the Civil War, it was never fully integrated into the larger city. Even on a map that doesn't mark it, Ohio City stands out because its street patterns run at odd angles that do not blend with the rest of Cleveland's street grid. For decades it was nothing more than a disintegrating neighborhood until the yuppies discovered restoring old houses could be trendy.

Helen had used some of the money from her divorce settlement to make a down payment on one of the old brick houses on Bridge Avenue. Later, when we met and I moved in with her, she had put me to work restoring it bit by bit. The money was hers. The manual labor was mine. That had been the period of my life when I had been laid off, when Linda had left me, when I was working only occasionally for Moe Glickman. The work on the house had been my therapy, something to keep me occupied and to give me a sense I was doing something worthwhile with tangible results. I had built new kitchen cabinets, stripped the old paint off the woodwork, chipped out the old horsehair plaster, lowered the ceilings, and done a lot of other chores to justify my keep.

And that's exactly what it was. Still is. Helen's salary as an associate professor of English at Cleveland State has always amounted to more than I could grub up. We had met shortly after my layoff, when I had invested some of my savings in tuition to pick up a few more credits toward my degree. Professor Scagnetti had been teaching a course in the argumentative essay in which she found merit in some of the acerbic pieces I wrote, saying I had a style reminiscent of George F. Will and William F. Buckley, who were my models. She also said my handwriting was atrocious. To cure that and boost my grade, she taught me to use her word processor and thus showed me her new house. Looking it over, I had pointed out what needed to be done, mentioning that I could do most of it and letting it drop that I was unemployed.

She was the teacher, ten years my senior, and I was her student. She owned a house, and I was about to be evicted from my apartment. Moving swiftly over the next steps: Our romance developed, we went to bed together after the term ended, and I moved in with her. We solved our financial arrangements by simply never talking about them. I contributed what I could to the general coffers, did the manual labor, and satisfied our mutual sex drives. Make of it whatever you want. It was simply the way I was living.

When I got home that afternoon, Helen's Honda Accord was already parked in the driveway at back. I crossed the patio and entered the house, searching for her. She was in the downstairs room we had converted into her study, tapping away at her word processor. "Hon———" I started to say, but she held up a forefinger and tapped out a few more words, frowning at the green phosphorous letters on the screen. Seeing her like that, I had one of those instances of recognition that hit me once every few weeks. I'll see her every day without giving it much thought, then suddenly see her at a certain angle or in a certain slant of light and want to gasp at the realization of how lovely she is. Not with the over-perfected beauty of a movie star or a fashion model but the attainable dark, mobile good looks of her Italian heritage. Say I'm prejudiced in her favor all you want. I've seen the reaction often enough from other men, seeing her walk into a restaurant, to know my estimate is supported by independent evaluations. For the few seconds I stood looking at her, my expression must have resembled the faces of those other men.

When she had completed her thought, she stood up and slipped her arms around my neck to give me a hello kiss that went beyond a simple greeting peck. When she broke from that, she returned to her seat in front of her word processor. She had already changed from her teaching clothes into a pair of jeans that clung nicely to her curves and to a blue chambray shirt that couldn't conceal the twin bulges of her breasts.

"What are you working on?" I asked.

"That piece on Hardy for the *Kenyon Review*."

"Stan Laurel and Oliver?"

"Thomas."

Helen's coffee cup on the table by her letter-quality printer stood empty. I took it into the kitchen and filled it, along with one for myself. Because neither Helen nor I drink, our Mr. Coffee machine gets a lot of heavy use. Carrying the coffee

back to her, I thought about her current project. In the middle
of last quarter, the professor of Victorian prose had suffered
a stroke that was going to leave him disabled for a long time.
Helen had inherited one of his classes in the novel. At the
same time, she had been receiving strong hints from the
tenure committee that she was overdue for publication. The
paper on Hardy was her attempt to stretch her research for
her lectures into double duty.

Understand that I'm only parroting what she told me. I
don't understand what half of it means, so I might have it all
wrong.

When I returned, Helen had turned her back on her word
processor screen to face me. "Done for the day?" My working
hours were so erratic the question had to be asked even though
I was in front of her.

"I've got a tail job later. I have to pick up a subject at Hopkins
and see where she leads me."

Her dark almond-shaped eyes that are not quite Oriental
looked quizzically at me. "Then you'll be out late?"

"Who knows? Why don't you ride along with me? The extra
cover would be good."

Helen glanced guiltily over her shoulder at the CRT. "I really
have to get this done. Academically, it's life or death."

"Academic life is a contradiction of terms," I said to show her
I had picked up something. "An oxymoron."

"It's there but it's below the surface, like slimy eels in the
ocean depths, like the Loch Ness monster."

"Speaking of which, one of your colleagues is my client. Boyd
Lassiter."

She lit one of her brown cigarettes while she searched a mental directory for the name. Afternoon sunlight was striking her
hair at an angle that accented its mahogany highlights on a field
that usually appeared to be inky-black. "The economics man from
Baldwin-Wallace who struck it rich."

"You never told me he once made a pass at you."

"He did?" She struggled to recall the incident. "The time he tried to hit on me at that conference? It hardly qualifies as a pass. When he started cozying up, I told him I had a blond young stud half his age who's hung like a donkey."

"Guess that's why he kept trying to get me to drop my drawers."

"Seriously, what's his problem?"

"Marital. Would you know his wife, Renee?"

"I don't think I ever met her. Gossip has it that she's a lush, or worse, who has made some bad scenes at faculty parties."

I showed Helen the photo Lassiter had given me. She studied the face and shook her head. "I'm positive I never met her. Is that who you're going to be following?"

"Uh-huh."

Helen took another hard look at her screen. "Now I really wish I could go along. The satisfaction of seeing what she's up to would be worth the trip."

"The real reason I want you along," I told her with concern on my face, "is that I don't know what she might try to pull. She might lead me up a dark alley and then try to buy me off with her white body. She'll remove her clothes gradually, one piece at a time." I reached out and unbuttoned the top button on Helen's blouse. "One by one her garments will fall off until she stands naked—all because I'm a blond young stud who's hung like a donkey."

Helen slapped my hand away from her blouse. "Don't worry about it. In this weather your tool will freeze and shrivel."

"Let's test it. Let's go out in the backyard."

"You're insane."

"Then let's go upstairs to our warm bedroom."

"Hmm."

I loomed over her chair and kissed her.

She tasted it and shook her head. "No thanks. I have to get back to Hardy's concept of fate."

"Bitch."

"Uh-huh. But it gets my paper written." She swiveled her chair back to the writing machine.

"We'll see about that." I spun her chair back my way and lifted her out of it. She wrapped her arms around my neck, her face nearly touching mine. "Now see here, Scarlett, you've put me off for the last time."

Our lips met, teeth parted, tongues moved. Helen said, "I'll think about Thomas Hardy tomorrow."

6 I arrived at Cleveland Hopkins Airport a little after seven that night and turned into the short-term lot, picking a parking space as close to the exit as I could get. I had left home as soon as I was sure that the rush-hour traffic had cleared the freeways. Making love with Helen had fouled up my plans for dinner, so I was arriving early enough to grab a sandwich in the cafeteria.

When I had finished eating, I strolled out into the main concourse to check on the flight from Las Vegas, via Chicago. It was on time. I picked up a copy of *American Handgunner* at the newsstand and ambled toward the arrival gates. I passed through the metal detector, being unarmed except for the pictures in the magazine, and went on down to the gate where the plane would be arriving. Instead of stopping there, I went on to the next gate lounge to mingle with departures for Florida. It was quite a crowd this time of year, most sensible people leaving Cleveland for warmer climes. I settled into one of the plastic seats and read an article in which some jerkoff from procurement was trying to justify the Pentagon's reasoning in switching from the .45 ACP to the 9mm Beretta. His reasoning made me shudder for the nation's security.

Looking up in disgust, I spotted a Stetson jutting above the heads of the crowd waiting for arrivals at the Las Vegas flight gate next door. Someone moved, and I saw the face below the Stetson: Clint Pettibone, Bremmel's bodyguard. Before he could look my way, I had my magazine up again, shielding my own face. I let time pass until I was sure his Stetson was turned and slipped out of my seat to head for the nearest snack bar. Sipping a cup of coffee there, I still had an oblique view of the gate, not as good an angle as I would have liked but sufficient for my needs. Clint's Stetson was high enough above other heads to be seen from a long way.

The Las Vegas flight taxied up to the passenger chute and soon people were walking down the concourse from the gate, grim-faced as if they were concerned about next month's mortgage payment. Soon I saw the Stetson moving my way and concealed my body behind a post and my face in the magazine.

They passed me three abreast. Clint was on the far side, one hand in the pocket of a sheepskin coat. Nearest me was a stranger, a hefty man unaccustomed to his double-knit suit. He had the look of a once-hard man whose last decade had been spent in easy living that had developed his paunch but still retained his toughness underneath. I would have cast him as a Teamsters official or maybe a career cop.

Between them was the woman who had been shooting craps in the picture Bremmel had shown me. Her face was still animated, now by something closer to fear than greed. She looked furtively at the two men, each of whom held an arm as if they were escorting a prisoner. Renee wore a winter coat with fur trim and tried to match her stride to her captors'. I gave them a thirty-foot lead and fell in behind them, shoving my rolled-up magazine into my topcoat pocket, seeing them without looking at them.

They went down the main concourse past the metal detectors and out through the hallway of shops into the central lobby dominated by a piece of sculpture welded out of old Cadillac tail fins. Beyond the sculpture, they took an escalator down to the lower

54

lobby to baggage claims. While they went to the gate for the Las Vegas flight, I joined the crowd milling around another airline's claim area.

The man I thought might be a Teamster had the claim checks. While he entered the fence around the turnstile, Clint stood outside with Renee. His eyes were fixed on the sight of bags sliding down the conveyor belt onto the turnstile. Renee looked up at him, seeing his fascination, then looked over her shoulder at the doors to the outside. She was measuring the dash that would take her through those doors.

Or was I imagining something? Inside the fence, the Teamster official plucked a Samsonite bag off the turnstile and set it aside, waiting for something else.

Renee had shifted her weight while I watched the Teamster, putting herself slightly behind Clint. She waited, eyes fixed on his left ear. Clint was still intent on his partner's work. Renee took a step back and pivoted in a half-turn toward the doors.

Without turning his head, Clint grasped her wrist and pulled her back to her former spot. He spoke to her softly out of the side of his mouth. I saw Renee's face contort in a grimace. It was not the words that affected her. Clint was twisting her wrist, and she was too frightened to cry out. Clint smiled, enjoying the expression of pain on her face. About the time I decided to charge over to them, he let go, his point made. Renee rubbed her wrist and sulked, but she did not look ready to try another bid for freedom.

She was their prisoner, all right. I fought down my instinct to interfere. For the time being, at least, they were through hurting her. Best I kept up my surveillance and maybe figured out what was going on here. Clint's partner returned to them with the Samsonite suitcase and a garment bag. The three of them moved over to the door where the Teamster wedged Renee into a corner with the two suitcases blocking her way out. When Clint started to pull on a pair of gloves, I headed for the door, passing behind him in time to hear Clint saying, "—should have brought a coat, Fred."

"Who thinks of everything on such short notice?" Fred, the Teamster official, said defensively. "I ain't even owned an overcoat in twenty years."

Clint adjusted his Stetson and turned up the collar of his sheepskin coat. "Wait here with her. I'll bring the car around."

He stepped out into the cold. I passed Renee and Fred and went through the automatic doors before they had completely closed behind Clint. He crossed the driveway and rode another escalator up to the level of the parking lot. Down the center of the lot runs a long, narrow shed with a conveyer belt in its center for those not inclined to walking. The shed gave us shelter from the cold and wind. Near the far end, Clint pushed through a door that opened on to the man-made tundra of the short-term parking lot, striking out across it at a no-wasted-time pace of someone with a definite destination in mind. I followed on a parallel course two aisles of parked cars over. Clint paused only once to get his bearings before he honed in on a pale blue Cadillac de Ville. While he was intent on unlocking the door, I passed close enough to read the license plate on the back and memorize it. Ohio plate with a local Cuyahoga County sticker.

I went on to my own Chevy and started the motor to get the heater working but stayed in my parking slot. The Cadillac came by and exited the lot, but still I sat. Clint would have to circle around to pick up his friends and pass this way again on the exit lane. Lights were bright enough here for me to see the Cadillac approaching. I had time to smoke a cigarette before it reappeared, this time with two passengers. I timed my exit from the lot so that I was paying the ransom when the Cadillac passed. I fell in behind them.

Clint had a lead on me, but I wasn't worried. He would be jammed up in traffic trying to exit the airport driveway on to the freeway system. Sure enough, he was four cars ahead of me at the first traffic light. When it changed, we all headed for the freeway cloverleaf. Clint looped on to Interstate 71 headed north, downtown, and I cruised along behind him. Being a stranger in these parts, Clint scrupulously observed the fifty-five-mph speed limit, and for once so did I, making us the two slowest cars on the road. Even the Smokies don't start arresting under sixty-five and the Smokies don't operate in Cuyahoga County. When the Cleveland police make a speed arrest, ceremonies are held at City Hall in commemoration. Because there was no way to shout this information to Clint, he kept poking along.

Ten interminable miles of this brought us to the viaduct with the first view of the Cleveland skyline at night. Terminal Tower, the BP America Building, Erieview Plaza, were all brightly lit to give the impression of a city showing off its jewelry after dark. From this vantage point it was impressive. Only down among the buildings would you understand the waste of candlepower on deserted streets. Clint continued across the viaduct and down the Innerbelt ravine, passing up each chance for a downtown exit. We came to Dead Man's Curve, where Clint almost scraped the wall despite his caution, and rounded it on to the eastbound Shoreway. Already beyond Municipal Stadium, we passed Burke Lakefront Airport, the Muni Power Plant, Channel 8 television studios, and even Gordon Park.

By this time I thought I knew where we were going. The Liberty Boulevard exit was still closed, so we would have to go to Eddy Road to reach Bratenahl, thence to Lassiter and Renee's modest cottage. I was so sure of the destination I was already looking to get on to the exit ramp, but Clint stayed in the center lane. We continued east for another five miles, crossing the Euclid city limits, until we came to signs directing traffic to exit on to Interstate 90 to Erie, Pennsylvania. Clint followed those signs.

What the hell?

I stayed with him, casting a worried eye at my gas gauge—three quarters. At least I had enough to reach Erie, if that was our destination. I suspected something worse. Just beyond the I-90 cutoff was another exit, at Euclid Avenue, where there is a cluster of suburban motor inns. Probably they were taking Renee to one of them. Wrong again. Clint passed up that chance and continued the way he had been going. Erie, here I come.

We looped around another cloverleaf with Interstate 271, the main route through the eastern exurbs, but stayed on I-90. Just when I was resigned to a tour of the Keystone State, Clint turned off at an exit leading to Willowick, Wiloughby, and Waite Hill—even I get confused among them. Clint turned the Caddy on to a country road that ran past isolated houses set well back in groves of trees and very few commercial establishments. When I was least expecting it, he turned into a driveway bordered by two stone columns. A discreet sign identified the place.

CARILLON CLUB

Dining—Dancing

I let myself lag back as Clint drove the Cadillac up a curving blacktop drive through the forest of leafless trees. It ended at a white-columned building that might once have been a private home. When the Cadillac stopped in front of it, a valet parking attendant came down the steps to take over. Clint and Fred led Renee into the building. No one was carrying a suitcase. The Carillon Club looked like a nice place, but I couldn't imagine anyone coming all the way from Las Vegas for a late supper.

After the Cadillac had been whisked off, I pulled up into its place. Music hit my ears when I opened my car door. I stood there a moment looking for its source. Among the trees was a tower like an oil derrick from which chimes were playing. Which explained the club's name. I took a ticket from the attendant and went up the steps between the columns. Through a pair of glass doors, I saw Clint and Fred escorting Renee through an arch across a lobby. Clint and Renee had disposed of their coats.

I entered the lobby. To my left was a staircase with a velvet rope looped across its bottom supporting a sign that read MEMBERS ONLY. That didn't concern me because my quarry had not gone that way. Around the staircase, I found a coat check counter and shucked out of my topcoat before I headed for the arch through which they had gone. A headwaiter holding a menu the size of a shield was blocking my way.

"Your reservation, sir?"

Over his shoulder I could see the room was a restaurant with half its white-cloth-covered tables empty and not enough people at the others to account for cars outside. At one side was a piano bar. Pretending not to hear the headwaiter, I let my eyes wander until I spotted Renee and her two keepers reaching a corner table. The man already sitting there was someone I knew—Otis T. Bremmel.

"Sir? Your reservation?"

"I'll be joining the Bremmel party. I see them now."

Exuding confidence, I brushed past the headwaiter and began threading my way through tables, in no particular hurry now. Near the piano bar, I recognized "Rhapsody in Blue" being played and meandered toward it, glancing at Bremmel's table often enough to keep track of what was happening there. I climbed onto a barstool, listening to the music with my head half turned toward Bremmel's corner. A waitress came, took my order for a scotch and water, brought it, and took my money. Three dollars! No wonder I don't drink.

While I had been getting into position, the three newcomers had joined Bremmel at his table. He stood up in deference to the lady, and all sat down. The waiter arrived and took orders for drinks. Only Fred was interested in a menu, which he puzzled over. Conversation was going on among them, but I was too far away for eavesdropping. Renee simply sat in her chair watching and listening to the others, sipping her drink when it came. The men knew each other and had plenty to discuss. Renee didn't know them and didn't particularly like them. She was wary, waiting for something to happen.

People around me applauded, making me realize the music had concluded. For the first time I looked at the piano player who was standing up to take a bow. Bending over made his long hair fall forward so that when he raised his head, his face was covered. He used both hands to push the hair aside, letting me see his face for the first time. It was a young, gaunt face that couldn't bring itself to smile at the applause. He sat again and returned to the keyboard to start "Maple Leaf Rag."

I toyed with my drink, considering my next step. I could go on sitting and observing what developed, which might have been the wisest plan. The trouble was that soon Bremmel or Clint would recognize me. My best move was to meet things head-on. I got up and walked across the room to Bremmel's table.

Fred was shifting restlessly. "How long does it take to whip up a meal here?" he was asking as I drew within hearing.

"Patience," said Bremmel, who had an empty plate before him and a burning cigar in his hand. His thick accountant's glasses turned my way, and his eyebrows moved higher above the rims. "Well!"

"Fancy meeting you folks here," I said, stopping at the table. "And you, too, Mrs. Lassiter. I heard you were out of town."

Renee looked up from her drink. Before she could answer me her eyes had to shuttle to Bremmel for permission. "I came back."

"Boyd will be interested in hearing that."

She had no comment. Bremmel asked, "Are you here at his behest, Disbro?"

"I'm only relaxing after hours."

Someone else was approaching the table. As he moved into my peripheral vision, I thought it was a waiter, probably because he wore a tux. Another step and I saw he was more important than that.

"Otis, sorry to keep you waiting. Business won't stop." He paused behind Renee's chair and looked over the group, finding my face the only one he couldn't approve of. The newcomer was a trim man probably in his forties, although the age could have been off a decade in either direction. His features were lean and taut over his bone structure, the kind of face that matures fast and ages slowly. His tan was not the complexion indigenous to northern climes in January. His hair was dark and wiry, tinged with gray at its edges, but his minimalist mustache was still black. His eyes were two drops of engine oil on the garage floor. In the right uniform, he could have been president-for-life of a Central American nation.

"Do you know Gil Disbro?" Bremmel asked.

"Afraid not." He was studying me as if he would be quizzed later on details of my appearance. If he had known me, he would have remembered it.

"Disbro is a private investigator hired by Mr. Lassiter to check up on his wife," Bremmel explained.

The newcomer continued his cataloguing of my features while he identified himself. "Duane Lagrasso. I manage this place."

Sinister Nightclub Owner. It was a species I had thought died out in 1947. But that was thinking backward. Lagrasso was no anachronism surviving beyond his time. There was an actorish quality about him, a supporting player's ability to fit himself into a niche. He had sculpted himself to the role which fit perfectly into the film noir ambience of this place. I was belatedly realizing that the decor here was done in black and white. I had stepped into a time warp when I entered the Carillon Club.

Lagrasso leaned on the back of Renee's chair, transferring his attention from me to her. "So we meet again"—his caressing voice paused before the noun of direct address—"Renee."

She killed what was left of her drink before she looked over her shoulder into his eyes. "So this is what you bought with the money from the girls—Duane."

The implied insult that he had been a pimp didn't bother Lagrasso. He showed her some teeth too even and too white to be attached to his gums. Then he looked at Bremmel and communicated something without words. I thought the message would probably have been verbalized if I hadn't been standing there.

A waiter appeared behind Lagrasso holding a chair. He sat down without looking for it, confident it would be there before his buns required it. Now Renee was caught between Bremmel and Lagrasso.

She stood up. "I'm going—"

Lagrasso laid a hand on her shoulder, not very hard, and she sat down.

"Too bad you can't join us," Bremmel told me.

Lagrasso took out a silver cigarette case, popped it open, and offered one to Renee before he took one for himself. That case was one more prop that could as easily come from a Gestapo major. "Of course your tab is on me tonight," Lagrasso said. He lit Renee's cigarette with a lighter built into the cigarette case and then his own.

She turned her head away as she exhaled, long enough for her green eyes to meet mine. They were eyes that had seen the creature change under the full moon, but there was no creature here—only Bremmel and Lagrasso, Clint and Fred. As I stared at those eyes, I saw something more behind the fear—an appeal to me that screamed *Help!* in a silence louder than any word.

I wanted to do something, but Clint and Fred stood up, forming a wall that blocked my access to the table. Unless I wanted to make a scene that would end with me filling out Blue Cross forms, leaving was my only option. I did.

7

The piano bar had quieted down when I returned to it. The pianist had finished his set and was gone somewhere on his break, maybe to his dressing room if he had one. My drink was gone, but as soon as I reclaimed my stool, a new one appeared in front of me. I lit a cigarette and kept my eye on Bremmel's table.

Lagrasso and Bremmel were both talking to Renee, who acted like a suspect standing on her Constitutional rights. Bremmel was not pleased with the outcome. Lagrasso gave him assurances and then took Renee by her arm and led her out of the dining room back toward the front entrance. Stretching a little, I saw where they went—up the staircase labeled by the sign MEMBERS ONLY. Bremmel, Clint, and Fred stayed at their table.

After a decent interval I took to the stairs where they had disappeared. The velvet rope at the bottom of the staircase was no problem. I stepped over it and climbed the stairs to meet the real problem. He was standing before the door at the head of the stairs, arms folded like a harem eunuch, a blond *Übermensch* who looked as if he had been valedictorian of his class at the Scandinavian Health Spa. The white dinner jacket he wore did little to conceal what was underneath.

63

"Membership card, please," he said in a voice that could have been computer generated.

"Mickey Mouse Club or Junior G-Man?"

He smiled tolerantly. He was paid to take guff from the trade but not to admit unauthorized personnel. "Sorry. It's a requirement."

"I'm with the Bremmel party downstairs. I have an important message for Mr. Lagrasso."

The names conjured things with him. He knocked on the door without turning away from me. It was opened by his classmate, the salutatorian. "Take this gentleman to D.L.," the valedictorian instructed.

"But—"

"He's from O.B."

That made all the difference. The salutatorian let me through the door into an alcove with heavy drapes across the opposite arch. Noise like the disgruntled chants of aroused natives came from the other side. My guide closed the door and parted the curtains.

The smoky room beyond was a gambling casino supplying the carriage trade with craps, roulette, blackjack, a chuck-a-luck wheel, a couple of poker tables, and slot machines along the wall. It looked like a branch operation of Las Vegas and probably was. It went a long way toward explaining the connection between Bremmel and Lagrasso. My guide took me across the room to another arch covered by a curtain, parted it, and came to another door.

As he raised his fist to knock, other sounds came from beyond the door. The smack of flesh on flesh and a heavy thunk of something landing on the carpet. My guide winked at me, letting me know he found the sounds enjoyable, and then knocked.

The door was jerked open in irritation, showing us Lagrasso standing there in his frilly shirt, his tuxedo jacket missing. "What is it?" he snapped, not happy with the interruption.

"Message from—"

Before the guide could say any more, I pushed the door open, forcing Lagrasso to give ground as I entered. The room was a lounge that might have doubled as an office, with furniture arranged like a hotel lobby, one piece being a desk. I skimmed over it quickly, my eyes finding Renee half lying in a corner of the couch. Her hair had fallen loose and one side of her face bore the impression of Lagrasso's fingers.

"Proving what a tough guy you are?" I asked him.

He looked past me to his hired muscle. "How did he get in here?"

"He said Bremmel—"

"He lied," Lagrasso snapped. "Throw him out."

I ignored that and looked at the woman who was watching us as if she were observing a play performed in a language she didn't understand. "Are you all right, Mrs. Lassiter?"

She touched the side of her face and nodded glumly. "I guess so."

A heavy hand landed on my shoulder. "Let's go."

My instructors at the academy always hammered on one principle of street fighting—never think of striking one blow and hoping it will settle matters. Always think in a series so that if your first punch doesn't get him, your fifth might. That was the philosophical groundwork of the number I did on the muscle man behind me. I scraped the heel of my shoe down his shin on my way to stomping his instep. At the same time I dug my elbow into his sternum. Spinning, I drove a knee into his groin and as his head came down, I chopped the back of his neck with the edges of both palms. I got hold of the back of his head and pushed down as I drove my knee up into his face. That left a clear shot for a punch in his kidneys. As he straightened again, I sent an uppercut to his chin that slammed his head into the wall. I cupped my hand under his chin and pounded his head twice more. His heels slid out from under him, and he began sinking to the floor, maybe technically conscious but with the fight gone.

All these calisthenics had revealed the shoulder holster under the guy's coat. I yanked the gun out and pointed it at Lagrasso. He was watching me like a fight promoter sizing up a prospect.

"Your boy is trained to look impressive on the beach. Next time you should pick one who knows his way around street fighting."

Lagrasso inclined his head toward the piece in my hand. It was a true belly gun, a Chief's Special with its sights and hammer spur filed off and the front of its trigger guard cut away. "That won't get you anywhere in here. You would never dare use it."

"Better hope you're right about that because you're the one who gets buried if you're wrong." I looked at Renee who was still looking uncomprehendingly at what was happening around her. "You can leave now."

"Leave?" The idea seemed strange to her. She remained on the couch still lightly touching her bruised cheek.

Lagrasso gave her a few seconds to move, and when she stayed put, he observed, "The lady likes it here."

He was at least partly right. Having made my play to rescue the lady in distress, I was beginning to feel awkward waiting for her to accept my help. Sir Gawain never had these problems yanking damsels from the dragon's clutches. "She'll like it better at home. If she wants to come back, that's her business." I jerked a thumb over my shoulder. "Let's go, Renee."

She looked at Lagrasso as if waiting for his permission. It was a look I had seen before in my police days, when I had dealt with battered women. I had seen wives right after they had been punched around, afraid to say anything bad about the man's character even with the cops standing there, ready to protest if we arrested him, rushing ahead to bail him out if we took him in. Being beaten, for some women at least, becomes a strange way of getting the love they aren't getting any other way.

Lagrasso nodded to her and looked at me. "There are things going on here you don't understand."

Brother, was that a true statement. What should have been a two-second job, getting Renee off the couch and out the door, had already dragged on for a full minute or more. "She's leaving with me. There's no other way."

Lagrasso seemed to be working to keep a smile off his face, as if the joke would be on me.

"I'd better go with him, Duane." Renee got off the couch and picked up her purse.

Lagrasso's expression changed. There was no more benign

tolerance, only hate deep enough to start a blood feud lasting generations directed at Renee. "You're not fucking up my plans."

"You don't own me." She meant it to sound like a firm decla-ration, but her voice broke.

"I own as much of you as I need."

Renee came over to me and stood behind me, one hand on my bicep. "Let's go," she said in a voice only I could have heard.

I wiggled the belly gun at Lagrasso. "You escort us out."

He shrugged and led the way. Renee followed, and I came last, looking for some kind of trap. Between here and the front door were any number of chances for Lagrasso's gorillas to jump me. It was his turf and he had probably arranged for all kinds of security, which could have explained his attitude of unconcern. Still, everything went smoothly for us. Clint and Fred were in the gaming room, probably having come up when they found me missing. If Lagrasso gave them any kind of signal, it was not to interfere. Across the room. Out the door. Down the stairs. Claim our coats. Out the front door and claim my car from the valet parking. Lagrasso stood in the cold in his shirt sleeves until my car arrived.

"Call me later," he said to Renee in parting.

She had her mouth open to promise she would before she caught herself.

We got in my car and drove off. No sirens chasing us. No electric gates closing. Once I was clear of the Carillon Club, I started driving through side streets in an aimless pattern that took us generally north, toward Lake Erie. Renee had slumped in the passenger seat, devoting full attention to my hood ornament. Suddenly, she snapped her head around to me.

"My bag! It's in the Cadillac!"

"Piss on your bag. You've got more clothes at home than Imelda Marcos."

It wasn't a retort calculated to endear me to her but you have to remember that my patience was draining away. Renee slumped into her seat and went into conference with her own thoughts. I wondered at her strange docility. Knowing what I did of her, I had to consider the possibility she was high. I couldn't detect the signs. Since getting off the plane, she had had a maximum of two drinks, hardly an amount to show on a Breathalyzer. She could have snorted something during the long ride in the Cadillac, but when I had first seen her in the Carillon Club, she had been alert. The only thing left was the short slapping around she had taken from Lagrasso. She had known him before the meeting at Bremmel's table without being fond of him. So what had he said to her upstairs to make her beholden to him?

A sign saying Lloyd Road, which I knew would connect us to the Route 2 expressway, came up. I took it and headed west, back toward Cleveland and on to the Shoreway again. Renee held her silence, refraining even from an expression of gratitude. Soon the interchange for Lakeshore Boulevard came up and I swung toward the exit lane.

"Not long now," I remarked, "before you're reunited with your husband. Boyd will be waiting up for you."

From the corner of my eye I saw her swivel her head away from the hood ornament to me, showing a trace of panic at the thought, more than she had shown facing Lagrasso. She returned her attention to the hood ornament. "Do we have to go there?" Her voice had an invitation that hummed with promise of better destinations.

"Your husband is paying me. His instructions are to bring you there." I gave her a moment to absorb that bit of morality before I asked, "Do you want to give me a reason I should do something else?"

"Two reasons. Bremmel and Lagrasso. They're dangerous. They scare me."

"Me, too. So won't you be safe from them at home?"

"I left Boyd for good reason. I don't want to be tied to him any more than those other two."

"Then here's my deal. Go see Boyd. If you don't want to stay there tonight, you don't have to."

"That won't work."

"It's the best I can do."

Lakeshore Boulevard led us into Bratenahl back to Buckingham Estates, where all this had started for me that morning. I

drove up the private road and through the arch into the courtyard, where I stopped. The frozen rivulets from that morning's
car wash were still there. Lights were burning in several windows, including the one to Lassiter's study.

"Be it ever so humble, there's no place like home," I told her.

"Fucking mausoleum," she said.

I shut off the car and got out, going around to the opposite
side to hold the door for Renee. She stepped out into the cold
air and looked at her home as if she had never seen it before.

"Let's go surprise your husband," I said, and started for the
door.

"Hold on." She turned to face me, hands jammed in her coat
pockets. "Before we go inside there are a few things you'd better know. You're going to find them out soon enough." Her
breath left vapor trails in the air that quickly dissolved.

Noise behind me, the slapping of loose shoes on the courtyard pavement. I turned toward it and saw a figure running my
way. When he entered a rectangle of light from the windows, I
saw he was dressed in pajamas and a robe. The slapping came
from loose-fitting slippers. When he had crossed a dark spot and
entered the next rectangle of light, I recognized Tram, the Vietnamese houseboy. He was running as if he were covering the
last six meters of a marathon, puffing vapor into the air. He
stepped on one of the ice patches and pitched forward. I caught
him in time to keep him from falling on his face.

"You!" he gasped out, producing more vapor than words.
"Help! Please!"

Something no meteorologist ever recorded blew a chill wind
down my spine. "What?"

"Bad. Ver-ry bad."

Excitement was causing amnesia for his English vocabulary,
not that it had ever been extensive. "Where?"

He pointed to the house, which was surprising considering he
had come from the garage. I helped support Tram to the front
door, which was standing open, and led him into the hall, where
there was an old church pew beside the umbrella stand. I set
him on it to give him a chance to catch his breath. Renee, who
had followed us inside, shut the door.

"Where now?"

Tram pointed to the sliding doors to Lassiter's study, the only room in the house I had ever entered. I started for them and realized Renee's heels were tapping along with me. I stopped. "You better wait here." With Renee standing against the wall, I went on and opened the sliding panels. I stepped inside and looked it over. Things were pretty much as they had been before with the exception of the body on the floor midway between the desk and the fireplace. And the blood.

I approached the body, carefully avoiding the bloodstain which had soaked into the expensive carpet. I maneuvered around so my back was to the fireplace, and I could look the body in its face. It was Lassiter all right. He was wearing a cardigan sweater and the trousers to the suit he'd had on earlier. He was lying on his stomach, head turned toward the fireplace with his right cheek resting on the carpet. The damage had been done to his head. His hair looked as if he had spilled a bucket of red dye over it. Bone shards were poking through his skull and another substance that looked like cottage cheese was oozing out. Hunkering down near him, I scraped a thumbnail across his eyeball. No reaction. If he had managed to live through this, he would have been nothing of the man he had been before.

I touched his flesh, which was cooler than normal but well above room temperature. I tried flexing his fingers, which had not stiffened. He had been alive two or three hours ago. My watch showed 11:07. Say it had happened while I had been following the Cadillac from the airport.

I stood up and looked for the blunt instrument. On the floor between the body and the fireplace lay the small iron shovel that was part of the set of fireplace tools. The blade was covered with blood and hair fragments. On the spines of books on the shelves were teardrop-shaped blood spots. The killer had struck once to put him down and then repeated it several times. The spattering of blood on the bookshelves came from blood splashing off the shovel on the backstroke.

There was nothing more I could do here. I returned to the hall where Renee was standing and Tram was sitting. I walked up to her and got a solid grip on her shoulders. I said it quickly to get it over with, the way you tear off adhesive tape.

"Your husband is dead."

Renee's long lashes blinked over her hazel eyes. She swayed on her high heels, and her eyes rolled. Her forehead came down and hit my shoulder.

"Jesus! Jesus!" was all she said.

I walked her to the church pew and set her down beside Tram, waiting for color to return to her face. Tram was ahead of her now in the recovery process, breathing slowly enough to understand three consecutive English words.

"You found him?" When he nodded, I asked next, "Then you went out to the garage? Why?"

"Find help. Get Gruznik. What do?"

"Did you find Gruznik?"

"Bad. Ver-ry bad."

Previous experience had taught me to heed these words. I went out the front door, leaving it ajar again behind me, and walked out to the garage. The belly gun I had taken from Lagrasso's bouncer was thudding against me in the right pocket of my topcoat. I transferred it to my hand as I neared the garage, seeing one of the bays standing open. I slithered in cautiously and felt for the light switch. When it came on, I saw the two vehicles there—the Porsche and a battered old Plymouth. No Mercedes.

Among the tools on the workbench was a flashlight. I picked it up and used the beam to probe into dark corners and under the cars. Only the Plymouth had an oil slick. I went outside and used the flashlight to guide my way up the covered stairs to the chauffeur's apartment above. The door was not locked. I entered and began turning on lights as I checked each room. The furniture came with the place and showed the years of use by many servants. There was no more a personal stamp on it than there would have been on a motel room. I passed on to the bedroom. The closet held chauffeur's uniforms but no civilian clothes. There was no luggage anywhere. The dresser had most of its drawers standing open and empty. One black sock had fallen on the floor, the result of packing in haste.

On the wall was an old fight card from the Detroit Olympia Stadium that listed Al "Whirlwind" Gruznik in the bottom panel. On the mirror above the dresser was a bumper sticker that read:

LIFE'S A BITCH.
AND THEN YOU DIE.

On the bed was a gray metal cash box lying open facedown like a book that had been put down to mark the page. Damage around the lock showed it had been pried open. On the bedspread was a brown paper bank wrapper that once had enclosed five hundred dollars cash.

On my way back to the house, I tossed the belly gun into the trunk of my car to avoid problems when the police arrived. Renee and Tram were still on the church pew, giving each other comfort. Tram pointed the way to the nearest phone so I could call the police.

8 The uniforms came first to look the situation
over and decide they had a real problem on
their hands. They sent for their sergeant who assured them, by
God, that guy looks dead. He sent for cameras and fingerprint
equipment as well as an ambulance with its siren and red lights
going. The paramedics listened through a stethoscope and tried
the old mirror trick and made if official: By God, he was dead.
Before the scene of the crime could be contaminated further, one
of the patrolmen took photos while another measured the location of all articles in the room and plotted them on graph paper.

Last of all came Captain Matthew Riordan, who might have
been a uniformed officer—I wasn't sure Bratenahl had detectives—but had certainly been called out from his home. He had
thrown a sports coat on over a flannel shirt and still wore Hush
Puppies. He looked over the scene and then set up a command
post in the living room. He was approaching retirement age, a
tired man with sagging jowls and bags under his watery blue
eyes. The breast pocket of his sports coat held a leather sheath
for his glasses, which he played with more than he wore. He
looked so innocuous he made me wary.

Riordan set up shop on a couch with a coffee table in front of him for a desk. He laid a legal pad on the table and selected one of the half dozen ballpoint pens from his shirt pocket. He tried writing with it, found it didn't work, put it aside and tried another. With that one he printed "LASSITER" in block capitals across the top of the page. He laid his pens aside, took off his glasses, and laid them atop the legal pad, looking up-from-under so that the blood vessels at the bottom of his eyeballs were plain.

"Tell me what happened."

"I don't think it was suicide," I said, "or an accident."

"You're sure?"

"It's only preliminary at this point."

He picked up his glasses and put them on. He took another pen out of his pocket and made his first notation: "Not suicide or accident." He put the pen down and took off his glasses. "Want this to go on all night, or do you want to get down to business?" He didn't show any preference one way or the other, and I did know he was serious.

"I started working for Lassiter this morning," I began, and went on to explain what I had done all day. Riordan had started with me, probably, because the uniforms had told him I made the best witness. Tram had a language barrier, and Renee had gone upstairs to lie down. The more I talked, the more Riordan relaxed and listened. By the time I wound down, he was leaning back on the couch with his legs crossed, twirling his glasses by one stem. He interrupted for questions only a couple of times to clarify a point. When I reached the stage where I met Renee's plane, he put his glasses on and took out another pen to begin notes on the time element. When I was done, he leaned back again and put the notepad in his lap. He studied it and removed his glasses to study me.

"How long had Lassiter been dead when you found him?" he asked.

"Do I look like Sam Gerber?"

"You've been a cop. What's your guess?"

"Two hours, maybe three."

He nodded. "That pretty much squares with my guess. Eight-thirty to ten should cover the time of death. Did the wife's plane land on time?"

"Give or take a few minutes."

"And you had her under observation the whole time after that?"

"Except for five minutes at the Carillon Club."

Riordan replaced his glasses, studied his notes, and then took his specs off again. "When a married man is murdered, the first place you look is his wife. Even more so in this case where the stakes are so high. No children, so the wife's got to inherit most of the estate. Twenty, thirty million maybe."

I shrugged. "More than we'll make in our lifetimes combined. She was still married to him when he died, regardless of what she was planning."

"Except she has an alibi—you."

"Sorry. I didn't intend it that way."

"So we've got the chauffeur. Would Lassiter really have fired him because you decked him?"

"Gruznik seemed to think so."

"Lassiter tells him he's fired. They have words. Gruznik grabs the shovel and clobbers him. Next Gruznik steals the house money—several thou—and takes off in the Mercedes, leaving his own car, the Plymouth, behind."

"Back up," I said, fishing for a Camel. "How do you know he stole money?"

"You saw the strongbox in Gruznik's room? According to Tram, that cash box came from Lassiter's desk. At least that's what we think he said. Tomorrow I have to find a Vietnamese translator and get a full statement from him."

"He didn't see or hear anything?"

Riordan pinched the two stems of his glasses together and used the thumb of that hand to scratch his thinning, wiry hair. "It seems Lassiter gave him the night off, and Tram went to his room at the back of the house to study English. He wouldn't have heard anything back there. The only reason he found the body was that he makes the rounds every night at eleven to check the locks and set the alarms. Got any idea why Lassiter let him knock off?"

"Me." I lit up. "He was waiting for word about his wife."

"Figures." Glasses went on and off while he studied more notes. "This Audrey Carnahan. She might have been pissed if he took Renee back. If she came knocking on his door, he would have probably let her in. They argue about it, and she goes bananas. It's what happened to that diet doctor in New York."

"Thought you had Gruznik figured for it."

"He could still have come along later and found the body and helped himself to the money and the Mercedes. There's a difference between stealing and killing."

"Lots of times they go together."

"Yeah, Gruznik is our best bet so far." Riordan held his glasses up to the light to see if they were smeared. "I wonder if Harry the Wrangler, the stud at the dude ranch, could be Harry Winch, the guy with Mrs. Lassiter in Las Vegas?"

More than ever I was sure it would not do to try pulling a fast one on Riordan. "It's what I suspected, but there's no way of proving it from here."

"Something you should consider." He was giving me his up-from-under look again. "You provided such a perfect alibi for Mrs. Lassiter you should wonder if you had been set up. She wouldn't have had to waste her old man herself. She has enough money to hire it done while she's establishing her alibi."

"Could she have known her husband would hire a private cop to tail her?"

"She didn't need you. She had Bremmel, Lagrasso, and all their henchmen. You were a bonus."

I inhaled, considering his theory. "And who would she have hired to caress her husband's skull?"

"Winch."

The door opened and a patrolman came in with a strip of computer paper in his hand, which he passed to Riordan. He put on glasses to read it and shook his head. "Record on Albert K. Gruznik. Assault, strong-arm robbery, manslaughter. Connections to LCN when he's been a collector for a loan shark. Investigated RICO." He passed the sheet to me to see for myself.

I read it and showed off my knowledge of governmentspeak. "'RICO' is the federal racketeering section. 'LCN' is La Cosa Nostra."

"Speaking of which, do you have any idea who Duane Lagrasso is?"

"He runs a gambling dive out east."

"Outside my jurisdiction. He's a made man. Used to be a pimp in Vegas who branched out into other things. Providing girls got him in solid with some West Coast people. One of the old farts out there died in the saddle while he was throwing the blocks to one of Lagrasso's girls. Heart attack, they said, but the old fart's death at that time was awful convenient for some people. They expressed gratitude to Lagrasso by setting him up with franchises in Miami, Covington, and here."

"Dope, too?"

"It's possible. Gambling, dope. It's all part of the same conglomerate. You would be well advised to watch yourself." Riordan got up and led me to the door, signaling my interrogation had ended. "Best thing we can do is see what the coroner has to say about the time of death. I don't think it's going to change anything. I've got an all-points out on Lassiter's Mercedes. It's not the kind of car you would have a lot of trouble spotting."

When Riordan opened the hall door, Renee was standing outside. She was looking better than when I had last seen her. She had combed her hair and put on fresh makeup, including some to cover the bruise from the slap on her face. She had also had time to down a few shots that had restored the color to her face.

"Captain, I can't stay in this house tonight, not after what's happened. I've already packed a couple bags. Do I have your permission to go to a hotel?"

"You don't need it. Of course you may," he told her. "It's probably the best idea all around. My men will probably be clunking around for hours. Where will you be staying in case I need you?"

Renee seemed to be stumped by that one for a moment. "Wherever I can find a room this late."

"How about Tower City Plaza?" I suggested, naming the most expensive place in town. Renee could afford it now.

She nodded in agreement and directed her question to Riordan. "You couldn't spare a man to drive me? Getting a taxi this time of night takes forever, and I really shouldn't be driving."

"I can't authorize that." Riordan looked at me.

I said, "I'll take you."

Renee wasted no time getting her coat and two suitcases. While I waited for her, I peeked into the room where Lassiter had died. His body had been removed, leaving a chalk outline in its place. My client was dead, and I was out of work, except for a job I had in the morning with Wally Stamm, only a few hours away.

When Renee came down with her bags, I took them and carried them out to my car. Frost had formed on the Chevy's windows, costing us time while I waited for the defrosters to melt it off. As we left Buckingham Estates, Renee turned around in her seat to take a last look at the place through the rear window of my car. She gave an exaggerated sigh of relief. "Glad to get away from there. I always hated that place."

She settled in on her side of the car to study the sights while I drove back to the Shoreway and headed downtown again. At this time of the morning traffic was light so that the freeway stretched out ahead of us like the landing strip of a deserted airfield. If I had expected her to break down in hysterics, she wasn't doing it. She was acting stunned, as if she had been hit over the head with a blackjack. Knowing what I did about her, I had to wonder if she had ingested any strange substances while she had been upstairs.

I moved over to the left lane in preparation for the turn on to the Innerbelt, chancing a look at Renee. "You're playing games with some nefarious types," I told her.

She looked my way but the shadows in the car were too deep to let me make out her expression. "I've neglected thanking you

78

for all you've done tonight. For a few minutes back there at the Carillon Club, you looked pretty heroic, like something from a TV show."

"I was working for your husband. My main job was looking out for your welfare." I steered the car through Dead Man's Curve. "It still could be."

"What's that supposed to mean? Are you building up to some kind of pass?" Her voice suggested she wouldn't have found that totally objectionable.

"No pass. What kind of hold does Lagrasso have on you?"

She laughed in a way that did not sound healthy. "You really wouldn't want to know the details."

I wooshed up the exit ramp on to Superior. Compared to the metropolis that was supposedly the hub of life for two million people, the Shoreway had been jammed. "You're a rich woman now with more money than you'll ever need. Keep running with Bremmel and Lagrasso, and you'll be bled dry in a couple years."

"That would be my problem, wouldn't it?"

Saving people from themselves is something I'm not geared for. It takes too much patience and tolerance for frustration for me to be any good at it. I said, "The thought of seeing those pukes prosper is what gets to me."

I drove on to Public Square and circled around the statuary to pull up in front of Stouffer's Tower City Plaza. There were doormen and bellhops to take charge of her once Renee crossed the sidewalk. We parted there.

Renee stood for an awkward moment while they removed her bags from my car. "You're a stand-up guy, Gil. I really do appreciate what you've done, more than I can show. Sometimes people have to play out the hand that's dealt them, even if they would rather do something else."

She stretched up then and kissed me, putting more into it than propriety would have suggested for a recent widow, promising even better things down the road. She went inside the hotel, and I went back to my car, which was still running to keep the heater going. It was past one o'clock and I had an appointment at dawn.

9

Early the next morning—later that same morning, technically—I took a trip with Wally Stamm into the third world around Kinsman and East 125th Street, where we snatched Henry Goodfellow out of his girl-friend's bed. We cuffed him and dressed him and loaded him into Wally's Econoline which has been customized into a jail cell on wheels. We took him downtown, passing Fourth District Head-quarters on the way.

Booking our prisoner into the Justice Center took up most of the morning. By the time I had finished filling out the forms and swearing to the affidavits—Wally always leaves the paperwork to me, another reason he likes to have me along—I was dragging with only two hours of sleep in my biological savings account. No matter how many cups of coffee I drank, my eyelids kept sinking. I walked across West Third to Glickman's office while Wally cir-cled the block in his van to enter the parking lot.

Gladys was waiting to ambush me as I came through the door. "This came for you by special messenger. Hel-lo Federal."

It was a number ten business envelope no thicker than an ordinary letter, but in my condition, carrying it to my office was

80

a chore. I flopped into my chair and woke up a few minutes later wondering why I was holding a knife in my hand. Slowly I figured out that the knife was a letter opener and what I was supposed to use it on. The envelope contained a certified check for five thousand dollars and a handwritten note "From the desk of Boyd Lassiter." It said:

> For retainer and expenses on your trip
> to Reno. Speak up if you need more.
>   Boyd

It was too much, and the trip was unnecessary now. I locked the check away in my desk drawer, telling myself I would have to return it and send his estate a legitimate bill for the fifteen hours I had put in, plus my expenses. But not today. I informed Gladys I was going home to renew my acquaintance with my Sealy Posturepedic. She gave me the kind of expression people who have never worked nights reserve for anyone who sleeps during the day.

Helen was home by the time my siesta ended that evening. Lassiter's murder had not made that morning's *Plain Dealer,* and I had not seen her to speak about it, but she had heard about it on her car radio driving home. Now she was full of questions about what had happened. When I had given her the basic facts, she compared it to what she knew. "It sounds like something out of Dashiell Hammett."

"More like Agatha Christie—the big manor house, the corpse in the library, servants."

"Who do you think did it?"

"The butler. You see, he's really a major heroin king from the Orient who was using his job as a cover for smuggling smack down the St. Lawrence Seaway. His henchmen would deliver it on ice boats late at night, and Lassiter caught him. So he had to die."

Helen hated herself for listening to half of that before she realized her leg was being pulled. She hated me even worse for doing it. "Are you satisfied that the chauffeur is the guilty party?"

"No," I said, serious this time. "I don't see him using the shovel on Lassiter's skull. Gruznik might have socked him, even beaten him to death, but he wouldn't need a club."

"Did you tell that to the police?"

"Riordan can think things out for himself. No one is paying me to solve murders. In fact, no one is paying me for anything at the moment."

Realizing she was not going to get me to explicate the death of the man who had once made a pass at her, Helen announced, "I'm going back to 'Thomas Hardy and Fate on the Wessex Moors.'"

"Sometimes," I said because it was on my mind, "you have to play out the hand that's dealt you no matter what you'd rather do."

En route to her word processor, Helen paused and tilted her head. "Fate as a dealer of poker hands. Not a bad image for what happens to Hardy's characters. I might be able to use it."

"Fate has dealt me the role of paying for your dinner tonight if you can spare the time."

"If that's the hand that's being dealt, I'll have to play it out. Fate as a waiter bringing a plate of food. There's another idea." She went into the study.

Snow was falling the next morning, Thursday, when I drove to work. It was a wet snow that could easily have turned to rain if the temperature climbed a few degrees, laying barely enough cover on the streets to leave tire tracks. Light as it was, cars were spinning and slewing on hills and at intersections. I was glad to park and get into my office.

The only thing waiting for me was Lassiter's check. I calculated a bill for my time, mileage, and expenses for the work I had done. It came out to less than four hundred dollars, not a tenth of the check. When the bill had been typed up, I called Bernie Schaefer in the Clerk of Courts office to see if anyone had filed Lassiter's will for probate. No one had yet, and I didn't know which law firm he had used, leaving Bernie stumped for any way he could help me. He had, though, been talking to

Linda, my ex, and now he felt duty bound to try patching things up between us, no matter how often I told him it was over, kaput, toot finney.

When I had escaped Bernie's solicitous concern, I called Stouffer's Tower City Plaza to ask for Mrs. Lassiter's room. She had checked out. That was not unexpected. She had only intended to put up there for the night until her house was cleared of the detritus of the homicide. I looked up the unlisted number for Lassiter in my notebook and tried reaching her there, getting Tram's voice instead. We had an interesting exchange sprinkled with bits of English, the most germane piece of information being his insistence, "Not here." Even when I asked in a louder voice (on the theory that volume will overcome a language barrier or that English spoken loud enough is universally understood) his two-word answer did not change.

For once I was beginning to sympathize with Washington bureaucrats. Giving money away isn't as easy as you might think. The only connection I knew to Lassiter was North Coast Investments, run by Audrey Carnahan, so I tried calling there. I got an answering machine that told me the office was closed this morning due to a death. I left a message hinting I had information about Lassiter.

So much for that. Only one name was left in my notebook, the musician Steve Stockman. Of the three ways I knew to run down Steve Stockman's address, two would require some effort. I could go through the local musician's union, or I could impose on some of my friendships in the records bureau to sneak a peek at his arrest report. The third option was the one I chose. I looked him up in the phone book, and then I wrote his address down in my notebook, and then I went there.

At the west edge of Cleveland's downtown flows the Cuyahoga River, cutting a deep ravine with ninety-foot embankments. That chasm has always been the most significant fact of Cleveland's physical and moral geography. When the city was founded, there were two communities here—one on each bank—and even today they live in an uneasy truce. West of the river the neighborhoods remain nearly all white. East of the river, beyond the downtown buffer zone, are the black wards. The glue that holds the two parts together was set down in the valley, the Flats, where John D. Rockefeller built his oil refineries and Andrew Carnegie his steel mills. In recent years the great industries have fallen on hard times, and the factories that ran the city the way a boiler room runs a ship have gradually closed. It has become so bad that pollution of the Cuyahoga has dropped to the point you can no longer set it afire by tossing a lighted match into it. It actually flows, and you can cruise it on a tour boat. Gentrification has set in as investors have opened a series of boisterous night spots that choke Old River Road with swingers on warm summer nights. Besides the saloons, developers have begun a campaign to convert the grungy warehouses into condominiums. One of them was the home of Steve Stockman.

I followed St. Clair down into the Flats under the shadows of the high-level bridges where last night's snowfall had melted off. It had to. The street department never gets around to doing anything about it. I found a parking space near one of the columns supporting the Detroit-Superior Bridge and walked to the former warehouse.

Rubbing my cold fingers together, I entered the lobby—a mailbox alcove—and tried making one of them work to punch the buzzer labeled Stockman. To my surprise, I got an answer. "What is it?"

I spoke into the speaker. "My name is Disbro. I want to talk to you about the Laffer Curve Band."

The inner door buzzed and I pushed through. A lot of work had gone into cutting up the old warehouse, not unlike the work going on at Audrey's office. I found my way through the halls and up to Stockman's unit. I tapped once and the door swung open.

"Come in," he invited. He was dressed in a pair of shorts and held a mug in his hand. He turned, yawning, and padded back into his digs. "Gotta excuse me. I worked a late gig last night, and I just woke up. I'm not too swift."

I believed the part about the gig. He was the piano player I had seen at the Carillon Club. I entered and closed the door.

84

Stockman had stopped by a Naugahyde chair to set his mug down on a TV tray. Exposed in his shorts, his body was thin to the point of emaciation with ribs starkly outlined and bony arms and legs the size of broom handles. His hair was blond, cut in a style that touched his shoulders. He backed into the chair and picked up his coffee mug. He sipped, said, "Ah!" and smiled at me, holding up the cup. "The low end of the speed spectrum. Like some? I just made a pot."

"Why not?" At his direction I went into his kitchen, found a clean mug, and poured from his percolator. Back in the living room, I shed my topcoat and sports coat too. That left me in my sweater, which was still too much. The thermostat must have been set for Stockman's level of dress.

"You play a good piano," I told him.

He looked at me as if he were bringing me into focus for the first time. "You were at the Carillon Club last night—the guy who made some kinda scene upstairs." He thought about the scene, not quite able to fathom where it fit in.

"Before that I heard some good music."

"Schmaltz. The owner gives me this list of songs they used to write before they invented rock. It's not what I'd choose to play, but what the hell, he owns the place." Stockman brought himself back to my original gambit. He was not as flighty as he put on. "Up front, man, I gotta tell you the Laffer Curve is no more. We dissolved."

I shrugged. "Same thing happened to the Beatles."

"Only it happened sooner to us." Stockman took another hit from his mug, coming around now. His face was puffy from sleep, and his bloodshot eyes suggested a hangover. He looked forty right now but under better conditions, he might have been only a couple years past thirty.

"Nice place," I said, looking around. One wall was nearly filled by a floor-to-ceiling window that bowed out, giving him a view of the river where it flowed into Lake Erie. The lake had frozen over, melted, and frozen again with odd-shaped chunks of ice jutting up to give it the appearance of a moonscape. The living room had a dining L at one end and a winding iron staircase that probably led up to the bedrooms. Near the dining L was a well-stocked bar with a sign above it that said COKE—THE REAL THING.

"It will do." He got up and made his way to the kitchen to refill his cup. Upon his return, he said, "You don't seem all broken up over the band."

"I didn't say I wanted to hire them. I said I wanted to talk about them." I got my leather folder holding my state ID card out of my sports coat and showed it to him.

"Is that real? You're really a private eye?"

"Really," I assured him.

"Then what is this?" He took his seat and leaned forward, elbows on his knees. His eyes were wide awake now, wary.

I lit a cigarette and looked at him through the smoke. "A friendly little talk."

"I'll bet. About what?"

"Renee Lassiter."

He smiled as if recalling his high school sweetheart. "A crazy lady. Nice crazy, I mean. She's with it for someone her age."

"How long since you've seen her?"

"She was in the Carillon Club last night, same as you."

"Before that."

He counted back on his fingers. "A month, maybe more. She left town around Christmastime. Said she was going to split from her old man. No wonder. He's a drag. Worse than ever, now that he's dead."

"When exactly did you see her?"

"Exactly? Shit, I don't keep a diary. The day before she left. Two days, maybe."

I nodded, as if there were great significance in that statement. "That makes you about the last person to see her before she left."

"So?"

I let it hang. "Where is she right now?"

"Probably at her home in Bratenahl."

I shook my head. "I tried there."

"Then I wouldn't know." He reached for a pack of cigarettes on the TV tray beside him and managed to get one lit on the third match.

"If that isn't enough for you, you're welcome to try something else."

"Say what?"

"I'm no narc."

Stockman studied me for a while. "Say it plain."

"The reason Renee came to see you before she left. She wanted to stock up on nose candy. You sold it to her, just like you supplied her all along."

"You're outta your fucking gourd," he told me. "You think 'cause I'm a musician I gotta be a doper. 'Cause I wear my hair long. 'Cause I hang out with people who might be users."

"That's three good reasons."

"Man, if I ever was to do such a thing, do you think I'd talk about it with a stranger?"

"Why not? I'm not a cop. I haven't warned you about your rights. You could admit to hijacking an airliner, and it couldn't be used against you."

He wasn't about to be suckered into anything so easily. "The last time I spoke to her was at the place where I work now, the Carillon Club. Lots of people were around. Maybe a hundred. I could give you ten names offhand."

"Don't bother." I put my cigarette out in his ashtray. "The two of you would only have needed a few minutes to slip out to the parking lot. It wouldn't matter if there had been a thousand people around."

"Then there isn't any point in us discussing it."

Probably he was right. I put on my sports coat and picked up my topcoat. He followed me to the door, where I paused. "I'll leave like you want, but don't forget I gave you a chance."

"Get bent."

I stepped outside then while Stockman held the door, trying to look formidable. "And don't come back!" he said loud enough to impress his neighbors and slammed the door.

10

Gladys had left a "while you were out" message on my office door. Ms. Carnahan had called to inform me she would be in the North Coast Investments office after two o'clock. That left me some time to kill, so I went out to Wally's desk. He was out on the street, so I looked over the three skip jobs in his tray while Rolf nuzzled me, hinting for me to scratch him between his ears. Before Moe issues a bond, he requires a preliminary investigation into the subject's credit standing. Wally does those investigations, unless he is busy on other things, in which case I do them. Of the three skips in the file, I had done two of the preliminary investigations and recommended against going their bond in both. Moe had disregarded my advice, so here I was looking for missing felons.

"What can you say at a time like this?" I asked Rolf. He had no answer except to dally his tongue out like a fifth leg.

I took the files on the three skips into my office and started working the jobs by phone. Time can slip by fast when you're involved in that kind of work, and before I looked at my watch again, I had missed another lunch. I typed up progress reports on all three jobs so Wally would know what I had accomplished and returned them to his desk. It was time for me to see Audrey Carnahan again.

I tucked the check in my pocket and went out to mush my way through the snow to the Arcade up to North Coast Investments, where the male receptionist was waiting for me.

"Ms. Carnahan is not seeing anyone today," he informed me. "Besides the devastating grief she feels for the loss of Boyd Lassiter, she is simply overwhelmed with the details of loose ends in his business affairs."

"Is she the executor of his estate?"

"De facto, if not formally."

"I need the present whereabouts of Mrs. Lassiter. She wouldn't by any chance have left her address with you?"

He rocked in his chair. "As a matter of fact, she did. She has returned to Las Vegas."

"Before the funeral?"

He nodded slowly. "She called me here to tell me she couldn't face the publicity and had to get away for a while."

Audrey Carnahan came out of her office dressed in jeans and a red plaid blouse that looked as if it had been made from a tablecloth. A tendril of her hair hung loose over a face worn with grief and tension. "Wayne, we need replies to these—" She broke off when she saw me. "Is it after two o'clock already?" She looked at the wall clock, having as much trouble keeping track of time as I was. "What brings you here today?"

"I'm still looking for Renee."

"That bitch! Do you have any idea what a mess she left for me to handle?"

"Some. What was the idea of her leaving, anyway?"

"Beats me." She dropped the papers on Wayne's desk. "Let's go into my office."

I followed her there, shrugging to Wayne to let him know I didn't understand it any better than he did. Audrey shut her office door and examined one of her plants hanging in the corner. She broke off a brown leaf and dropped it in the wastebasket as she went behind her desk. "A cop was here asking questions. Captain Riordan?"

89

I nodded. "The investigating officer."

"Aren't the police looking for the chauffeur?" she asked. "Isn't he the one who killed Boyd?"

"He's the prime suspect."

Audrey drew out a cigarette and began tapping it. She was Joan Crawford again. "Riordan was asking me all kinds of questions about where I was Tuesday evening, as if I needed an alibi."

My respect for Riordan was unblemished. "You could account for yourself without any trouble, couldn't you?"

"I was at home working on some papers."

"Any visitors? Phone calls?"

"No visitors but my phone rang a couple times. I didn't answer it, though. I didn't want to be interrupted, so I let my answering machine take over." She lit her cigarette with shaking fingers. "I might have trouble proving I was there."

"What difference does it make as long as the police are after Gruznik?"

"I'm not sure. Riordan insinuated I would have had a motive for killing Boyd if he had taken Renee back. The way he put the questions made me feel guilty of something."

"That's the policeman's way."

She snorted out smoke and eyed me across her desk. "Your way, too, if it comes down to it."

"I'm unemployed. My only interest now is tracking down Renee so I can square off the last bit of business."

"Anything I can do for you?"

I stopped myself from reaching for the check. "I'd better talk to Renee. Do you have any idea where she's staying in Las Vegas?"

"None at all. I can't believe the way she simply blew town with nothing but a phone call to Wayne. Not even staying for the funeral. On top of everything else, I had to close the office this morning while Wayne and I made the funeral arrangements."

I reverted to an aphorism. "There's no telling how a person will react to grief. For some people death is more than they can face."

"That's Renee all over. She's never been good at facing up to the consequences of anything. Still, you'd think that even she could go through the motions this time. She doesn't have to be so hell-bent on spending the fortune she's inherited."

I clucked with her over the injustice of it all and left the office quickly but hung around the Arcade, stopping at the food court on the first floor behind the staircase to brood over a cup of coffee. The check in my pocket weighed as heavily as if it had been printed on lead. Why hadn't I turned it in? Greed was one answer. All I had to do was endorse it and deposit it in my account. Added to the reward money I had coming for Goodfellow's arrest, it made a nice nest egg that would allow me to coast for a couple months. But that wasn't it. The check represented money that Lassiter had mailed me from the grave, even if he didn't know that's what he was doing at the time, for services to be rendered in the future.

He had paid in advance for information which I was supposed to dig up on his wife. It was the bargain we had struck, and he had kept his part of it, depending on me to deliver soon. His death didn't cancel out that contract. Lagrasso had told me there were things about Renee I didn't understand, a point I agreed with more than ever. Her actions these past few days had been so bizarre that there were obviously unknown circumstances out West that were having an effect on her. Had Lassiter been alive, he would have been demanding I get to the bottom of it. Because I understood that much, I knew that returning Lassiter's check would have been as immoral as pocketing it. The only way I could purge myself was to earn it.

Before I left the Arcade, I stopped at a travel agency.

"Reno?" Helen asked that evening when I told her about it. "Why would you go there?"

"Because that's where it begins, the start of the trail, the scent of the convict's shoe."

She blew on her coffee and looked at me over the rim of her cup. "I don't think it's really necessary. You could keep the money."

"A man's got to keep the promises he makes. He does that or he's nothing."

"John Wayne?" She sipped her coffee and set the cup down. "I'll miss you for a few days."

"Come with me."

"To Reno? We're not even married. How can we get divorced?"

"We can lie out in the burning desert sun until our passion heats and then satisfy it in an air-conditioned bedroom."

"Only it won't work out that way. You will be gone all day and half the night running down leads, just like it is in Cleveland. Besides, I have responsibilities—classes to teach, exams to grade, research—"

"Call in sick. Tell them you have to go off to cure your herpes."

"—and the paper on Hardy. Don't forget that has to be done."

"A few days, a long weekend, will do you good. Nevada will remind you of Hardy every minute. The land is just like those moors in Wessex."

"There could hardly be two places in the world less alike."

"So much the better. The change will encourage creative juices to flow. Consider Nevada a laboratory where fate and gambling are playing out Hardy's hypothesis."

"Hmm." She was smiling now. "You just might have hit on something. Seeing the gambling, the desperation in the faces of the players bucking the odds, joy and depression. It might be worth something after all."

"You have to come." I whipped out the two airplane tickets. "We leave tomorrow."

"Impossible. I can't go on such short notice. It's out of the question."

11

The first thing Helen said when we got off the plane in Reno was "It's cold."

She was wrong. The temperature was in the mid-fifties, making my tweed sports coat about right. She meant it was not the baking hot temperature she had been expecting. I might have been responsible for some of her disappointment by overbilling the climate.

"That's harsh talk for someone from Cleveland. If we had a day like this there in January, people would start seeding their lawns." I draped my topcoat over her shoulders. She was wearing a sleeveless summer blouse and had put her winter coat in her suitcase, beside our swimming gear, as soon as we were inside the airport back home.

When we had claimed our baggage, I headed for the car rental desk. They tried to set me up with a Chevette, but I told them to save it for Doc, Grumpy, and Sneezy. I'm a full-sized man who deserves a full-sized car. I drew a Crown Victoria. I loaded our baggage into the trunk and drove into Reno. As we cruised down Virginia Street looking for a place to stay on a weekend without reservations, Helen watched the flow of people, intent on finding fodder for her paper on this Hardy who was not Stan Laurel's partner.

All the way out from Cleveland she had been discussing gambling and had probed for my sentiments. "I've never seen you gamble, not even buy a lottery ticket."

I thought about that. "I don't think I ever have."

"You don't bet on horse races or prize fights or football games."

"Or elections or the stock market."

"Why not?"

"I don't know." I stared at the white head cover on the seat ahead of me, trying to come up with a reason. "It isn't something I ever thought about. It's one of the many things I don't do along with fishing and sky diving and playing golf. It's always been illegal. When I was growing up, I always wanted to be a cop. I never ran with people who gambled, and I just never did it. You don't gamble, either."

"That's my upbringing. My parents were children of the Depression. They were Catholic, but they didn't attend Bingo Night—not from moral objections but because they thought it was frivolous. Any extra money they had, they saved in tin cans buried in the garden. They thought it was risky enough putting it in a savings account. There's more of my parents in me than you might think."

"You don't bury it in tin cans."

"But I look upon gambling as foolishness. Not immoral, maybe, but unwise. Anyone who gambles will lose eventually. Besides, there were other influences on me when I was growing up in the old neighborhood. I heard about losers who were badly beaten. Some men were pointed out to me as being enforcers, some of them the same men who came to collect the protection money Dad paid for his store. These were the same men who formed the subculture I've been trying to live down most of my life."

Talking about it like that had made me realize I had missed nothing by not gambling. Now I turned into an adequate-looking motel within walking distance of the casinos. We stayed only as long as it took to register and drop our bags in the room before we went out to find a restaurant. It was noon here but late afternoon by my watch, which was set to agree with my stomach. On our way out of the restaurant, I took a quarter from my change and dropped it in a slot machine. Nothing happened.

"Waste," Helen said, and we went out to stroll down Virginia Street. I found a drugstore that sold a street guide for Reno and the surrounding area and a directory to dude ranches. The Triangle K was north toward Pyramid Lake. When we reached our motel, I gave Helen one more chance to come with me. She preferred staying in town to see the sights.

I got into the rented Ford and drove through a lot of empty country to the Triangle K. It had a big main house of stone, a bunkhouse for the crew, and another building with units like a motel for guests. There were barns and corrals and other places I couldn't identify. I parked out of the way and walked over to the corral where a group of people stood hanging on the corral boards, watching the horses mill around inside. They were all leathery types in big hats and cowboy boots. One of them was a woman.

She turned and looked my way. "Help you, stranger?"

"Howdy," I said. "I was looking for the boss lady of this here spread."

It had sounded like an appropriate opening to me but it drew guffaws from the wranglers at the corral. Maybe something about the way Joel McCrea delivered it made it sound more natural.

"That's me, pard." The woman stepped forward and put out her hand. "I'm Viola Kravitz." She could have been any age over fifty, no more than a couple inches over five feet, buxom in a man's Western shirt and heavy enough to put strain on the rivets of her jeans. Her hair was red, leaning toward pink, and done in pigtails. Her face had never been handsome, but it had seen a lot of life and usually found a joke buried in it somewhere.

"Gil Disbro." We shook hands.

She glanced over her shoulder at the wranglers who were down to snickers. "Pay them no mind. What did you need from me?"

"I wanted to talk to you about a woman who was staying here a couple weeks ago, Renee Lassiter."

"You're not a reporter?"

It struck me as a strange question. "I'm a private investigator from Cleveland, working for her husband. He claims he talked to you on the phone the other night." I brought out my ID case as evidence I was telling the truth.

"Sure did." She glanced back at the wranglers and then nodded to the main house. "Let's go up there to talk."

As we walked toward the stone house, I looked around some more. "Nice place."

"Shit! Would you know a singletree from a diamond hitch?"

"No, ma'am."

"Then you don't know whether I've got a nice place or a buffalo wallow."

"That's about right."

"So don't try to soft-soap me on things you know nothing about. Butter me up on subjects where you're an expert. Here, we'll set on the veranda."

It looked like a front porch to me. Viola Kravitz dropped into a wooden captain's chair, hooking a leg over an arm and putting her own arm over the back. I settled into a rocker.

"For a man whose wife is leaving him, this Lassiter seems hell-bent on keeping track of her," she observed.

"Lassiter isn't paying me to figure out his reasons. He just wants his wife found."

She nodded approval of my answer. "I don't know what to tell you. One day she was here, next day she wasn't. She brought along enough things to last her six weeks, but when she left, she took only what would fit into one suitcase."

I recalled that Renee had bought a lot of things in Las Vegas with Lassiter's credit card. "Wasn't that about the time you lost one of your hired hands?"

"Honey, that was the day everything happened." There went

another of her cryptic remarks, like asking if I were a reporter. "But you're right. His name was Harry Winch. He took off for no reason, too."

"That ever strike you as more than coincidence?"

"Sure. It also struck me that two things can happen on the same day without being connected. You really have to understand Harry. He never was a professional wrangler. Lately he's been promoting real estate around the south end of Tahoe. He has an office in Stateline on the California side and an A-frame up in the mountains where he used to live. Either business went sour when a deal fell through, or the law got hot on him. That's when he came to me for a job to tide him over. I knew him from the ranch I used to run outside Vegas, and I put him to work, not expecting him to stay forever. If he got word a prospect was ready to be fleeced or the law had forgotten him, he would have gone back to Stateline in a minute." She stood up. "You Easterners don't drink much coffee, but I'd sure like some. You're welcome to a cup if you want it."

"Black," I said.

She went inside and returned with a Corning Ware brewer and two mugs. She plugged the coffee pot into an outlet on the veranda, poured coffee into both mugs, and took hers back to her chair.

"I understand Harry had a way with your female guests."

"He's a gigolo." Viola brought out a pack of Luckies and struck a wooden match on her boot sole to light one.

"He got friendly with Renee?"

She inhaled and blew smoke out while she considered it. "Women come out here to spend time waiting for their divorce. Some of them take it hard, like the breakup of their marriage is proof of their failure as a woman. That kind needs reassurance. A man making a pass at a woman like that is proving she's worth something after all. That was the value of having a man like Harry around. He could reassure lots of women. Renee Lassiter, though, wasn't one of them."

The last statement hit me like a rabbit punch because it contradicted everything I knew. Or maybe not. When Bremmel had

97

told me Winch and Renee were living apart, I had assumed it was part of their cover. Maybe they really had no interest in one another, and the scam they were working—whatever it had been—was strictly business. Or maybe their joint appearances at the tables had been as coincidental as their joint disappearance. I wasn't ready to accept any of that.

"I'm not saying he never made the moves on her," Viola was explaining. "I'm sure he did, and maybe they sneaked off for a quickie. It sure wasn't anything that would make them run off together and start a new life. Renee had another interest, another one of the women living here, Shana Tracey."

The rapidity of surprises was making me feel a little punch-drunk. Viola must have seen it in my face because she added hastily, "Nothing queer. They were good friends, like sorority sisters, except I don't know what sorority sisters are like. Renee and Shana were two of a kind who enjoyed being around each other. They were so close to the same size they could wear each other's clothes. They had the same interests, the same likes and dislikes. Shana had a car, a Rabbit, and they'd take off together to go into Reno for the action at night. Once a friend, a woman from back East, stopped to visit Renee, and Shana let her borrow the car to go to the airport."

"Do you know who the friend was?"

"Not by name. Renee told me it was her husband's mistress. Renee thought she had a lot of nerve coming here to spy on her."

"And what do you know about Shana Tracey?"

"Just about everything." Viola tapped her cigarette ash over the veranda railing. "Sweetie, I told you I ran a ranch down by Vegas. What kind of ranch do you think it was?"

"Brothel?"

"A licensed whorehouse. Shana was one of my girls then. There was a man, Homer Tracey, who was one of her regulars, a widower close to sixty who owned a ranch with mineral rights he'd sold to a mining company. He proposed, if you can believe it, and Shana decided to leave the life. They got married and it lasted a couple years, until last month. When she moved out on him, she looked me up and rented a unit here while the divorce went through."

"What happened to her marriage?"

"Search me." Viola flipped her cigarette butt away. "It could be Shana never adjusted to married life. It could also be she married Tracey for his money, expecting him to die soon. He got a good price for the mineral rights he sold. Nothing like Howard Hughes but enough to make life comfortable. Shana could have decided settling for half was better than waiting for him to kick off."

"Is Shana still here?"

Viola looked at me strangely. "You didn't know? Maybe not, being a stranger here. Shana is dead."

I stared at her until I realized I'd been doing it for too long. "Since when?"

"They found her body Monday." Viola stood up and went inside again, returning with a series of newspaper clippings. "I saved these. They will probably explain things."

I took the clippings and skimmed through the headlines, seeing they had come from successive days earlier in the week. The headlines, in order, summed up the stories:

UNIDENTIFIED WOMAN'S BODY FOUND

BODY IDENTIFIED: SHANA TRACEY

COCAINE CAUSED SHANA'S DEATH

The news columns below the headlines expanded on the information. On Monday a family out riding their dune buggies in the sagebrush had come across the badly decomposed body of what the coroner later determined had been a female Caucasian, thirty-five to forty, five six, 120 to 130 pounds, with auburn hair. The body was down at the bottom of a ravine five miles from the nearest highway and nearly three from the nearest access road. No marks of violence were found, but vultures and coyotes had damaged the body beyond immediate recognition.

On Tuesday the paper reported that a Volkswagen Rabbit had been found parked on the access road near the body's location. It was registered to Homer Tracey of Tonopah, but Deputy Sheriff Farlow Hudspeth refused to speculate whether there was any connection with the dead body.

On Wednesday, Hudspeth was less reticent. He announced that the body had been identified as Shana (Mrs. Homer) Tracey. Besides the car, deputy sheriffs had located Shana's purse halfway between the car and the ravine. They had also located Homer Tracey living temporarily in Sparks. He had identified the remains based upon the clothes and jewelry she had been wearing. Tracey, sixty-three, a retired rancher, stated his wife had been on vacation at a local dude ranch. He further stated he had moved to Sparks to be near her. He denied they had been legally separated.

On Thursday, the coroner announced the cause of Shana's death was cocaine poisoning. She had been dead approximately a week when found. The coroner reconstructed the sequence of events leading to her death.

Shana had driven a friend, Renee Lassiter, from the Triangle K to the Reno airport to put her on the plane for Las Vegas. Somewhere during that trip, Shana had ingested the cocaine that eventually killed her. En route back to the Triangle K, Shana had begun feeling the ill effects. She pulled off the highway on to the access road to rest, or perhaps simply was confused. The coroner speculated that once the access road ran out, she had begun walking. Cocaine has the effect of making the user hyperactive, he explained, so she may have felt she could walk the rest of the way. She lost her purse on her journey. By the time she reached the ravine, the combined effects of cocaine and exercise put too much strain on her heart.

Deputy Hudspeth had no comment on the coroner's analysis. He reported he had attempted to contact Mrs. Lassiter in Las Vegas only to learn she had gone back to her home in Cleveland.

"Wait until the newspapers find out Shana was a hooker, and

I was her madam," Viola predicted. "Shit's really gonna hit the fan. Just because it's legal here, whoring hasn't become respectable."

"Where did the coke come from?" I wondered.

"I'm not a narc spying on my guests. I wouldn't permit its use up here, but anyone could get away with it down in their room."

"How would it get here?"

"They could bring it with them, they could get it in Reno, a visitor could bring it." She shrugged at the endless possibilities.

"Winch could have supplied it?"

"Not likely. One thing I never knew him to be involved in is dope traffic. It was always too big a rap for him to face. If he did it, it would be as a favor to one of the women. Even then he would most likely take her into Reno and introduce her to a connection so he could stay out of it."

"Did Renee ever mention a man named Duane Lagrasso?"

"Not Renee. Shana knew him, though." She recognized renewed interest in my face and explained, "He was Shana's pimp when she was working the streets, before she came to my ranch."

I tried imagining the permutations contained in that morsel. Renee had a link to Lagrasso in Cleveland through Stockman while Shana's connection with Lagrasso went back a few years. Recently the two girls had met on this spread—to compare notes on Lagrasso? He had told me I didn't understand half of what was going on. I was inclined to think half was a high percentage.

There were many more questions I could have asked Viola, if I had known what they were. I needed time to dope out the facts I already had. I said farewell to her and headed for my car. Before I pulled out of my parking space, I took down my map of Nevada and looked up Tonopah, halfway between Reno and Las Vegas. A man who owned a ranch near there could go to either of the two major fun centers for relaxation.

As I was starting my car to pull out, a sheriff's cruiser came down the road leading from the highway. It stopped and the deputy got out, a lanky man in a Stetson and khaki uniform with a green bomber jacket. He paused to expectorate a brown stream and hitch up his gun belt, taking note of my rental Ford. When he spotted Viola on the veranda, he touched the brim of his Stetson. "Afternoon, Viola," I heard him say.

"Howdy, Farlow," she answered.

He walked around the front of his cruiser toward the house. After that, their voices were pitched too low for me to make out their words. I knew a cure for that. I switched off my engine and walked up to them.

12

"—asking in my official capacity," the deputy was saying as I climbed the stairs to the veranda. "I've got to know where that cocaine came from."

"Hell, Farlow, that makes no difference to me," Viola answered. "Official or friendly, my answer is the same. I run a dude ranch, not a prison. Grown-ups here can do pretty much what they please, come and go when they want. Lotsa substances could be in their rooms without me knowing."

The deputy had turned his head toward the noise of my approaching footsteps. He was a big man with lots of time in the saddle whose face was like basket-stamped leather and whose mustache had been inherited from Wyatt Earp. The name tag pinned to his jacket read Hudspeth, the same as the investigating officer in the Shana Tracey case.

"Who are you?" he asked in a tone of voice that encouraged straight answers.

I told him and backed it up with my identification. "I was about to come see you about Mrs. Tracey's death anyway."

"Who's paying the freight?"

Put that way, the question gave me no moral compunctions

103

about my answer. "Boyd Lassiter, Renee's husband. When he hired me, he told me he was concerned about his wife's welfare."

"With good reason." Hudspeth turned back to Viola Kravitz. "I'm going to have to take a look at Mrs. Lassiter's room."

"I don't think I can let you," Viola said.

"A couple days ago you let me go through Shana's room," Hudspeth pointed out.

"That was different. She had died." Viola looked at me. "What do you think?"

"Depends," I said noncommittally. "What is the fact situation? Is her rent paid up?"

"Through next week."

Hudspeth's faded-denim eyes were regarding me critically as I said, "Expectation of privacy is the key here, wouldn't you say? As long as the rent is paid, the tenant has claims to privacy. When the rent expires, the control of the premises reverts to the landlady."

"You're no lawyer," Hudspeth said, not sure of his statement.

"I have to know the laws of search and seizure, same as you." I spoke to Viola, "Better require a search warrant or wait until the rent expires."

She nodded. "I think that's what I'll have to do."

Hudspeth's gaze told me I should not consider myself his buddy. "You better understand how serious this is, Viola. There's good reason to suspect the cocaine that killed Shana Tracey came from Renee Lassiter. This could be a murder charge."

"Where do you get that idea?" Viola asked.

"From the sworn statements of two men in Reno the girls met in a bar. Renee invited them out here for a toot."

Viola frowned, trying to dredge up a recollection. "They came here?"

"Not that night. The men had coke of their own to snort in town. Renee would have been paying them back, see? But before they could collect, Shana was dead and Renee was gone."

"Chickenshit," I judged. "The most you have is hearsay evidence that Renee might have had nose candy in the room. Even if you could prove that and also prove that Renee gave the fatal dose to Shana, you still don't have a murder case. Involuntary manslaughter would be stretching it."

No sooner were the words out than I sensed I had said exactly what Hudspeth wanted. The inverted V of his mustache flattened out as his mouth beneath it widened into a smile. "Yesterday I would have agreed with you. That was before the coroner's office ran some tests on Shana's hair and her fingernails. The tests were positive for arsenic. That's something you don't normally find in coke."

His point made, Hudspeth spat a stream of tobacco juice over the veranda rail. "Now I'm asking you again, Viola—will you let me search her room?"

"Nothing has changed. If the crime is all that serious, that's all the more reason to do things right."

"Thought you might see things that way." Hudspeth reached into his jacket pocket and withdrew a paper—a legal document on foolscap folded into four sections. "I took all this to the judge, and he gave me this search warrant."

Viola read through it and handed it to me. "What do you think?"

I read it, having seen enough search warrants in my lifetime to know what to look for. Nevada's forms were not that different from the ones used in Ohio, all being pretty much dictated by the Supreme Court rulings. This one gave Hudspeth the right to search unit 7 at the Triangle K in daylight. The signature was indecipherable but probably authentic. "It looks all right."

"It's a command from the court to do it," Hudspeth expanded. "I can kick down the door if I have to, but you won't make me do that, will you, Viola?"

"You have a right to go with him," I advised Viola. "He has to leave a copy of the search warrant and an inventory of any property he seizes."

"That's right." Hudspeth shifted his cud to the other side of his mouth, still not ready to be my buddy. "Why don't you come along, too. Then you can testify I didn't plant anything."

Viola led us down to the guest rooms and unlocked the door

to number 7. It reminded me of a standard motel room with Western touches—an overhead light fixture that looked as if it had been made from a wagon wheel, a set of longhorns over the door, an antler hat rack. There were no bodies. I had reason to know Renee was still alive, but it had occurred to me that Harry Winch might also have snorted a line of the contaminated cocaine.

Hudspeth tossed the room thoroughly, making sure I was able to see every place he looked before he touched it. When he would open a drawer, he would stand back first to let me see. As a result, I learned as much as he did. Renee had left little of value behind, unless her clothes were so expensive their worth added up to a lot. Some clothes were in a laundry bag ready for the wash. More clean things still hung in her closet. The medicine cabinet in the bathroom held a nearly empty tube of toothpaste, a disposable razor, and two minipads for those light days left in a Handipak. No jewelry. No arsenic.

The white powder we suspected was cocaine was in a clear plastic bag taped to the back of the dresser. Hudspeth dropped it into an evidence bag and sealed it before me. "Cocaine laced with arsenic," he predicted.

"You can tell that already?"

"My best guess. The gas chromatograph will bear me out."

There was room to argue with him, but my own instincts told me he was right. Hudspeth filled out the return on the back of the search warrant, left a copy and an inventory listing the bag of white powder. "Satisfied?"

"With one more thing. I'd like to see the dead woman's body."

"Why?"

"My client would expect it of me. After all, his wife is missing, too. He'd want me to assure him there's no mix-up."

Hudspeth's mustache flattened out again, as if he had a secret. "Sure. Glad to."

Promising to lead me to the morgue, he drove back to Reno while I followed in my rented Ford, pacing him at seventy mph. That speed knocked off a third of the time the trip would otherwise have taken me. In the morgue he led me into the room where the bodies were stored in refrigerated file drawers. Hudspeth stopped at the one he wanted and pulled it open. Her body was outlined under a sheet like the Bride of Frankenstein.

"You ready for this?" Hudspeth asked.

"As much as I'll ever be."

Hudspeth pulled the sheet back to expose most of her body. I had been wrong. She was in worse shape than the Bride of Frankenstein. The newspaper accounts had told me she had been attacked by vultures and coyotes. The results were plain enough. Her eyeballs had been picked out and chunks of flesh had been ripped from her face and her body. I spent some time going over what remained, noting that her fingernails had been removed.

"You did that?" I held up her hand to Hudspeth.

"To get the samples to test for arsenic." Disappointment was showing on his face because I had not keeled over. "How long were you a cop?"

"Nearly three years."

"Where at?"

"Cleveland. We spent a lot of time at the morgue under Lester Adelson." I looked her body over some more, hunting for an identifying scar. "The newspaper accounts said the body was badly decomposed. That bothered me because arsenic preserves the body."

"'Badly decomposed' was the paper's choice of words. They're as good as any."

"You took her fingerprints?"

"We still haven't got a kickback from Washington. You should know how long that takes."

My first stop was a sink where I could wash my hands. Hudspeth closed the drawer and headed for the front of the building. When I caught up with him, I found him at the front desk with an unshaven man wearing soft and faded Levi's—pants, shirt, and jacket. He was over sixty and held a stuffed grocery bag. Coming down the hall, I had heard his slurred voice arguing with the morgue attendant. Hudspeth seemed to be trying to deflect the man's anger.

"You can have her back soon, Homer. We need her a couple more days to be sure, is all."

"She deserves a decent burial," the man said, halfway to tears.

"We're counting on you to see to that, Homer. A couple more days won't matter."

Homer. Homer Tracey, Shana's husband, I surmised. He wore a baseball cap with John Deere on its front.

"God, how I loved her! This shouldn't of happened to her."

"You're all worked up," Hudspeth said solicitously. "Why don't you sit down and rest a spell?" Gently, he guided Tracey toward a wooden bench. "You still staying at your place in Sparks?"

Tracey nodded, walking with a drunk's unsteady stride that worked to avoid tangling his feet. "She didn't have to die like that."

"I know. We're doing our damnedest to get the people responsible."

Tracey half fell onto the bench, hugging the grocery bag to him. The top item in it was a manila envelope with his wife's name printed on it in Magic Marker. The bag would hold her personal effects with the smaller items in the envelope.

"You don't have to stay here," Hudspeth was telling him. "You can go back to Tonopah. We can make arrangements to have Shana shipped to you there."

"I'll have her cremated here. I'll take her urn back with me."

"Whatever you say but that's the reason, see, we don't want to release her too soon. Anyway," Hudspeth went on, "you should go back home. You've got a place to look after."

"Piss on it!"

"You don't mean that. Hell, Shana wouldn't want you to talk that way. She'd want you back there tending to your stock."

I lit a cigarette and leaned against the wall, watching and listening. Hudspeth was building to something.

"God knows, ranchers around here wouldn't dare be away as long as you've been. We got problems with predators up here. Don't you have the same thing in Tonopah?"

"Some." Tracey shook his head. "I don't give a shit no more."

"How do you handle predators in those parts? You can't cover your land fast enough to shoot more than a few of them."

Tracey rocked, squeezing the bag. "Put out some bait."

"Poisoned bait? The Sierra Club types don't like that."

"Fuck them."

Hudspeth's cud changed sides, a sign the zinger was coming, I was learning. "What do you use?"

"Arsenic."

Hudspeth's eyes searched me out to see how I was taking it. I nodded. Simply because Renee was his prime suspect, he wasn't passing up other possibilities.

Tracey tried to stand up but lost his balance and fell back. "Goddamn it."

"Where do you think you're going?"

"Back to my place." Tracey stood up, only to sway unsteadily.

"You're in no condition for that," Hudspeth told him. "You can't drive."

"I drove here."

"Homer, you try to leave, I'm gonna hafta arrest you—for your own good."

"I'll see he gets back," I volunteered. I took Tracey's arm and steered him down the hall toward the exit door. Hudspeth came after us and called me back. I leaned Tracey against the wall and retreated a few steps so Hudspeth could talk in low tones.

"Pump him all you want but let me know if he makes any admissions, hear?" He thought about it all and added, "I can loan you a tape recorder if you want to capture what he says."

"No thanks. I never have any luck with those things." I looked down at Tracey and tried to imagine him on trial for poisoning his wife. "You really believe he could have killed her?"

"I turn over every stone I come across."

"What would his motive be?"

"Sometimes a marriage license has the motive for murder

written into the fine print." Hudspeth looked at Tracey. "Shana was a whore working at Viola's place down in Vegas when she met him. Why would a whore marry a man like that, except for his money? He had sold off mineral rights to the mining interests then, but lately the market has played hell with the mines. When they shut down, the royalties quit coming in, so Shana left him. Tracey saw he was gonna lose her anyway, so he's got nothing to lose by killing her."

I looked at Tracey, so drunk he could hardly stand by himself. "Hard to imagine him as a killer."

"That's what I thought until I checked his record. When he isn't on a jag, he's no one to screw with. He spent time in Special Forces in Nam. Last year he nearly got in trouble when some guy, who used to be one of Shana's customers, saw her and started making remarks. Tracey tore into him and nearly put him in the graveyard. Only thing that kept Tracey from jail time was a good EMS unit that brought the customer around in time. Tracey got off with a fine for assault."

"I guess it makes more sense than trying to lay it on Renee Lassiter. She had barely met Shana."

"They knew each other for a month or more," Hudspeth pointed out. "Something could have come up between them. Maybe jealousy over Harry Winch, just to make a wild guess."

Hudspeth out here and Riordan back home were closer than the miles between them would suggest. I wouldn't have wanted either of them on my trail. Renee Lassiter had them both.

Tracey had lurched away from the wall and was making obliquely for the door. I left Hudspeth to rush after him before he could do harm to others or himself.

13

Before I could get Tracey into my car, he insisted on going back to his pickup truck, which was parked outside at a crazy angle. He spent a solid five minutes searching his pockets for the keys and when he finally found them, he unlocked the passenger door and went to the glove box for a pint of Wild Turkey. It calmed him the way a bottle pacifies a colicky baby. While he was getting it out, my eyes noted another object that had been keeping it company in the glove box—a Ruger Security Six in stainless steel. When Tracey turned away from the pickup to drink from his bottle, I slipped the gun out of the glove box and into the waistband of my pants under my coat.

Tracey made it to my car supporting himself by working his way along the hood to the passenger door. He bumped his head twice getting in and sloshed whiskey on the seat. When I was behind the wheel, I said, "You're going to have to tell me where to go."

"Sparks." He took another slug and I started heading east on Fourth Street. "Who the hell are you, anyway?"

"The name is Gil Disbro. I'm a private detective from Cleveland looking for Mrs. Lassiter."

I wasn't sure any of that had registered on him. He drank more and looked at the afternoon traffic moving from one casino to another, a strange mingling of East and West. "Ever been in the Army?" he asked.

I confessed I hadn't.

"I was. Enlisted when I was eighteen and worked my way up to master sergeant. Put in my twenty and got out. Then I settled on my ranch that I bought with my savings." Tracey reviewed the tape of his career in his mind. "There's an old Army saying: 'Whores make the best wives.' Do you know why that is?"

"Because they really know how to please a man?" I ventured.

"It's because they really know how to please a man," he told me, proving there was no need for me to worry about sparkling repartee on my end. "Trouble with that is you never know. You never know if you're making her happy or if she's faking it. That's her business, making johns happy. You never know."

"It's the same way with any woman. How do you know if she's faking it or not?"

Tracey's head turned in my direction, as if I had revealed an insight that unlocked the key to the universe. "That's right, ain't it? You never know with any woman. Do you understand women?"

"No."

Tracey brooded some more as we crossed the line into Sparks. "All women are whores," he concluded. "Especially married women. Just 'cause they only fuck one man don't change nothin'. Husband provides his wife with a place to live, groceries, a paycheck. She fucks him in exchange. A wife is a whore under a different name."

Profound philosophical depths I didn't want to probe too deeply, thinking of my own relations with Helen. "I need some directions."

"Two lights, turn left. You been listening to what I said?"
"Sure."

"You shouldn't. I'm full of shit." He drank more bourbon. "Know what's wrong with it? I left out love. That makes the difference. When two people live together out of love, they don't consider it a business deal. They just do things for each other because they want to."

"You loved Shana?"

"Sometimes. And sometimes I hated her for being a whore. I never wanted to think about that while we were together, but it was there in the back of my head. There were times I wanted to kill her."

I followed Tracey's directions which took me on to a residential side street that petered out into a gravel road at the city limits, where it ran between houses that looked as if they would be inhabited by people whose luck had petered out like the street. One of the last ones was a shack that seemed to be clinging to the tower of its television antenna for support. Tracey had me stop at it.

Getting him out of the car was twice the job getting him in had been. I supported him across the barren yard to the cement blocks that led up to the door. There was no front porch or even a veranda. The door was unlocked, suggesting there was nothing inside worth stealing. I guided Tracey across the threshold and pointed him to the nearest piece of furniture, a couch leaking its stuffing. He made it without spilling his pint.

With Tracey safely settled, I looked around. The house had a bare cement floor with Navajo throw rugs scattered between pieces of furniture, most of them wrinkled as he had stumbled and slipped around. Articles of clothing were draped haphazardly over chairs and light fixtures. The television set was on, tuned to an afternoon talk show with celebrity guests who were promoting their shows in Vegas or Tahoe. It made no difference to Tracey. To him, the television set was a form of moving wallpaper.

The shack had a bedroom and a bathroom to one side and a kitchen in the back. The bed was unmade. I went into the bathroom to take a leak, checking the medicine cabinet while I was at it. Nothing that looked like arsenic. I moved on to the kitchen where a trash can filled with fast-food containers was attracting flies. On the table was a plate of half-eaten beans that fed another family of flies. The sink held dishes that had been scraped clean but never washed. I found a jar of instant coffee, filled a tea kettle, and put it on the gas range to heat.

Out of Tracey's sight, I took his revolver from my pants and opened the cylinder. It was loaded with round-nosed .38 Specials, two of which had dented primers. I dumped the brass into my palm and saw that two cases had been fired. The four-inch barrel showed bits of lead and powder in the grooves, and there was powder residue on the cylinder flutes. I tossed the rounds into the garbage and concealed the revolver on a high shelf in the kitchen cabinet. Much as it went against my grain to take away a man's piece, Tracey was in no condition to be handling it. He was the kind of man who could give the antigun lobby more fodder to justify passing laws that would take away my guns.

Back in the living room, I found Tracey playing with the remote control to his television. He had hit an unused channel that filled the screen with meaningless sparkles, which satisfied him as much as anything. I wondered if I were in the home of a Nielsen family.

"You were telling me how you met Shana," I said.

"I was?" He raised the bottle to his lips and partook. "We met at Viola's place in Vegas. I was living in Tonopah and I'd make excursions down to there. I was married when I retired from the Army, to a Korean girl. She died six years ago, some Oriental disease. Then along came the mining companies to dicker for my mineral rights, and suddenly I had more money than I knew what to do with. I started running down to Vegas when I felt the urge for some nooky. It's legal here."

"I know."

"Shana was one of the girls. Pretty soon I started asking for her special. Next time she had a vacation coming to her, I invited her to my ranch. She came and looked it over, and I told her about the royalties from the mines. Then I proposed and she accepted."

The sequence of events as Tracey ordered them portrayed more about their relationship than he understood even as he told it. "Could a girl like Shana be happy on a ranch?"

"The first year for sure. It was like a long vacation to her, being away from everything. She learned to relax, not to do anything, a rest cure." He leaned his head back on the couch and watched a spider crawl across the ceiling.

"Had she been using dope?" I asked.

"Some, sure. Pot and coke, mostly. She wasn't hooked on it, and once she got on the ranch, she didn't need it. She went a year and a half without touching anything except booze, and not much of that. Even when we went somewhere where folks might offer her some, she turned it down. That's why I say life on the ranch was good for her."

The tea kettle had begun whistling. I went into the kitchen to shut it off and found two clean cups on the shelf—clean except for accumulated dust. I rinsed them out and dumped an extra portion of instant coffee into each one, added boiling water, and carried them back to the living room.

"Try that," I offered, putting the coffee before him.

"Who needs it? I've got this." He lowered the level of his bottle, which was nearing bottom. "It works, sooner or later. I forget."

In an attempt to keep his memory going, I said, "Did Shana start snorting coke again?"

"A little, now and then, toward the end. She never had a problem with it, but it still killed her. Like them football and basketball players you hear about. One snort and you're dead, if it hits you wrong."

I pulled up a straight-backed chair that looked as if it might not collapse on me and sat in it the wrong way, leaning forward on the back. "That's when she was getting ready to leave you?"

"Yeah. I guess it was a sign of what was coming. One day she told me she had to get away and come up here to start divorce proceedings. No fault of mine, she says, it's just the way it was. I followed her here, rented this place over a month ago. I thought I could talk to her, change her mind, at least be here. Lot of good it did me. Christ, this fucking place is a shithole."

"You could clean it up."

"Why bother? It's what was available when I was looking for

115

a place to stay. Without her, it doesn't matter. Nothing matters anymore." Tears leaked out of his eyes, etching through dirt on his face and through his bristly gray whiskers. I looked away from him, sipping my coffee, letting it pass. After a while, I looked into my cup. "Did you ever help Shana?"

He sniffled. "What do you mean?"

"Get her any coke?"

"I wouldn't know where to start. That bitch she was friends with was the one that done it." He looked at me again. "Did you tell me that you're looking for her?"

"Yeah."

"You find her, let me know."

"Why?"

"I don't know. Sometimes I want to kill her. Sometimes I don't give a good goddamn."

More than ever I was glad I had emptied his gun and hidden it. Tracey was at a point where a violent outburst would be a release, whether he turned it upon others or himself. Thinking of the two empty cartridge cases, I wondered if he already had.

"Why are you so sure Renee Lassiter provided the cocaine?"

"She had it. Shana told me so."

"When did you talk to her?"

"Lots of times. We'd run into each other in Reno. Truth be known, I'd follow her around. She didn't mind. I think she kinda liked having me there. Every once in a while, she would let me catch up, and we'd have a drink together or something. It was one of those times she mentioned about the other woman having a stash any time she wanted some."

"Did Shana say she'd ever snorted any of Renee's cocaine?"

He made a heroic effort to dredge up the memory from his alcohol haze. "I think she'd had a toot. I'm not sure."

It wasn't the definite answer I'd been hoping for. Even if Shana had ingested previous doses of Renee's cocaine with no ill effects, it would have been no proof the cocaine was pure. The effects of arsenic over a period of time can be cumulative. I had another angle to pursue. "Were you following Shana the night she died?"

His head dropped. "I tried. I waited down the road from the Triangle K, but she didn't come out. What happened was, I fell asleep in my truck. I'd been drinking. She must have passed me while I was out. After I woke up, I drove to the ranch and saw her car was gone. Jesus! If I'd just followed her that night, maybe things would have been different. Maybe not. At least she wouldn't have had to lay out in the open like that until the animals got her."

He started crying again, racking himself with deep sobs this time. It was time for privacy. I left him to go out to the car for the grocery bag filled with Shana's belongings. Tracey had fallen into a drunken sleep when I returned. I set the bag down and went through it, finding nothing that surprised me. The dress she had been wearing had been shredded by the animals. The envelope contained her jewelry—wedding band, engagement ring, necklace, bracelet, watch—none of which were cheap but nothing to compare to the rocks Renee had worn. I put everything back in the bag, leaving it for Tracey's mementos.

Before I left, I got a comforter off the bed and brought it into the living room to spread it over Tracey. He stirred and opened his eyes. "I lost her. I lost everything. I got nothing left." Strangely, he laughed. "I got one thing left after all. The cancer. Did you know I'm dying? I never told her. I didn't want her to pity me. If I had told her, she might not have left me. She would have stayed until I died."

I stayed with him a few more minutes until he fell asleep again. After that, I left.

14

When I got back to the motel, Helen was waiting for me as if she had been planning a surprise party. "Gil, look at this!" She pulled me into the room and pointed to the bed. The spread was covered with money, bills laid out as if in a giant hand of solitaire. "Look at that!"

"Where did it come from?" I asked.

"I won it!" Helen bounced up and down, a look burning feverishly in her eyes. I had last seen that look in the photo of Renee at the crap table. "I played a slot machine! I pulled a lever and all these quarters came tumbling out! Seven hundred dollars! I had to convert it to cash because it was too heavy to carry." She bounced some more.

"Don't be silly," I said, patting her firm round tush. "You're not built to play a slot machine. You don't have a size twelve ass to stuff in a pair of size six Capri pants."

"Seven hundred dollars!" she repeated in case I had missed it. "Do you know how many papers I have to grade to earn that much? How many classes I have to teach? How many lectures I have to prepare? And I won it all in the time it takes to pull a lever down."

"How many times?"

"Well, it took a few but not that many. Ten minutes at most."

"I thought you were here to observe gamblers succumbing to their fate, or something."

"I know. I asked myself how I could observe them without knowing something of their sinking feelings. I decided I had to play."

"Fine. You made seven hundred dollars. Now take the money and run."

"That's what I thought, too. That's what I did."

"Great."

"Now I'm having second thoughts. This is found money, their money."

"It was theirs. Now it's yours."

"Listen, Gil, I'm having a run of luck, beginner's luck. If I take half the money—just half of it—and put down some more bets, I could win again. I'd double it, triple it."

"Keep it up," I said. "Pretty soon you're going to know that sinking feeling all gamblers feel when succumbing to their fate."

Helen shook her head. "You don't understand. This wouldn't be gambling. It would be more like investing."

"Oh, investing. Now I understand."

"You're being sarcastic."

"Skeptical. I have to run down to Stateline. Would you like to come along?"

"What is Stateline?"

"A little town at the south end of Lake Tahoe, half in Nevada and half in California. There's gambling on the Nevada side of the street. I have to see a man down there and then we can have dinner somewhere on the way back."

"How far is it?"

"A half hour drive."

Apparently Helen decided she could wait that long to test the tables in Stateline. While she gathered up her money, I advised her to bring a coat because we were going into the mountains.

We headed south on the freeway toward Carson City, which the guidebook told me was the smallest state capital in the country. That surprised me, being familiar with Columbus, Ohio. Maybe it was reserved for the title of Most Parochial. Helen noted the exit signs along the way. "Silver City. Virginia City. Carson City. It sounds like a marquee of old Warner Brothers oaters."

Helen lowered her head to the pad in her lap, on which she was calculating her winnings if she only risked part of her loot at two-to-one odds. I held my peace as we entered Carson City. The half hour I had predicted for the trip was already used up, with another twenty-five miles to go. It was largely uphill as we climbed to the shore of Tahoe. Then we entered Stateline.

Winch's real estate office, in a building converted from a gas station, was on the California side with a CLOSED sign on the door and an OFFICE FOR RENT sign in the window. Also in the window was a sketch map showing the way to Winch's development site on the lake: Ponderosa Acres. I traced over the map and set out for the area in the hope that the A-frame Viola had mentioned was up that way.

Ponderosa Acres was well marked by signs that had been vandalized by the weather or teenagers or disgruntled investors. The road brought us out on a cleared plateau staked out in lots. There was no view of Lake Tahoe. I stopped and we got out, Helen in her hooded lined trench coat. We stood on the plateau and watched the sun sinking over the horizon like a golden Frisbee.

"Due west"—Helen pointed—"is Steinbeck country."

"Southwest"—I pointed—"is L.A., the spiritual home of every private eye."

I moved around, scanning the surrounding woods until I spotted a building among the trees. It was an A-frame with touches of Swiss chalet. "Let's see if we can find a way to that."

We drove back to the road and headed in the direction of the A-frame. A mailbox by a private road was labeled: H. Winch. I turned there and followed the road, twin ruts, uphill, curving around trees and bouncing in chuckholes the size of meteor craters. The road leveled off at last in front of the A-frame. I parked and got out, Helen following tentatively in the dust the car had raised just now catching up with us.

"It looks empty," she observed.

I went forward anyway, feeling the chill twilight wind blowing on me. I climbed onto the redwood deck that served as the front porch (veranda?) and rang the bell. It *bing-bonged!* inside to no effect. I walked around the deck and peered through the windows that formed most of one wall. Furniture, showing no wear, arranged like in a model home. I went on around the house, trying doors and windows, all of which were locked. Garage doors under the house stood open, showing me it was empty, but offering an entrance to the house.

The door leading from the garage into the house was locked, a simple arrangement where the key fits into the doorknob, one of the least burglarproof arrangements imaginable. With a nail file I borrowed from Helen's purse, I managed to spring it open in under three minutes. Not that it did me any good. The inside was absolutely bare of any sign of human habitation. It was set up as a model home with furniture strictly for display purposes, with paper runners laid down to protect the carpet. If Winch had ever stayed there, he had cleaned up after himself. Closets and drawers and shelves were totally empty.

"All this for nothing," Helen said, shivering despite her warm coat, when I emerged again.

"At least I know now he isn't here." My eyes were on the ground, making out twin ruts bending down the grass, looking like tire tracks. They led across the yard to a grove of pine trees.

"Ready to go?" Helen asked.

"I'm going to follow these." I headed for the trees, where darkness seemed to be an hour ahead of the rest of the world. There was still enough light for me to see the rear end of a bronze Mercedes ahead with an Ohio license plate and a Cuyahoga County sticker on it. A lot of road dirt had splashed on the car since the last time I had seen it.

I went along the left side and saw the bulk of the man behind the steering wheel. He wasn't moving. I rapped my knuckles on the window. He still didn't move. I tried the door handle and it opened, turning on an overhead light that let me see the face I knew as Al Gruznik. The back of his head was matted with a sticky substance such a dark red it was nearly black. The bullet had entered behind his left ear and exited under his right eye. It hadn't happened while he was sitting in the car. The trajectory of the bullet would have damaged the windshield or scattered more blood on the seat. There was none.

I touched him, feeling cold flesh like marble. Rigor was pronounced, jaw tight and head rigid. I guessed he had driven across two thirds of the country in less than three days in a car on the hot list—which probably shows how much attention the list gets from most police agencies—and been killed shortly after his arrival here. Earlier today. I moved some hair and tried to get a fix on the bullet hole. Too small for a full-sized caliber, too large for a .22, no sharp edges for blunt-nosed ammo that would probably have shown on flesh stretched tight over the skull. That left the medium-range family of calibers. The exit wound didn't seem to be consistent with 9 mm or .357. That left .38 Special, .380 auto, or possibly a .32. The .38 round-nose bullets from Tracey's Ruger, which I had held in my hand a couple hours ago, would have been about right, unless this had been done with a rifle. But Tracey's gun had had two rounds fired.

A twig snapped behind me and I turned to see Helen standing beside the left rear tire. Her face was whiter than the winter complexion called for. "That's a man in there."

"So it is."

"He's not moving."

"He's not likely to."

"He's—is he—" She couldn't bring herself to pronounce the verdict.

I tried diplomacy. "Let's say he won't be counted in the next census."

She swallowed as if she had strep throat. "Who is—was—he?"

"Al 'Whirlwind' Gruznik, ex-boxer and currently Boyd Lassiter's chauffeur. This is also Lassiter's Mercedes. The presumption a couple days ago was that Gruznik murdered Lassiter and stole his car. It looks like he drove it out here—"

"—and killed himself," she finished for me.

"No, someone had to do it for him. Let's get out of here." I closed the door of the Mercedes and hustled her back to our rental Ford. Headlights were needed as we left Winch's house and drove back down the road to the highway. I reached Stateline and passed through, heading back toward Carson City.

"That gas station back there had a phone booth," Helen reported. When I made no effort to turn around, she asked, "Aren't you going to call the police?"

"I don't think so."

"Why not?"

She wanted an answer that would line syllogisms in neat order while I was operating on gut feelings. "The body is in California but he wasn't killed there, or even in the car. The murder might have taken place in Nevada. The motive is floating somewhere between Cleveland and Las Vegas. There are too many jurisdictions involved, too much to explain to the law."

"They can sort all that out."

"They can do it without my help. In fact I don't know what to say to them. I don't understand why Gruznik came here from Cleveland, or why he was killed, or what all this means to the assumptions we all made about Lassiter's murder. I need time to sort those things out. I also need time to figure out how this affects my client's interests."

"Your client is not going to be counted in the next census, either," Helen pointed out.

"So in a way I'm working for his widow, who inherits his interests. Except she may be at cross-purposes to what her husband wanted. Of course, she might have shot Gruznik if Harry Winch or a man named Homer Tracey didn't do it."

Confounded, Helen shook her head. "Most of what you're saying might as well be in a foreign language."

"Then forget all that and think of Gruznik as what you gamblers call a hole card. I know he's there, you know he's there, and one more person knows he's there."

"The killer."

"So maybe he or she will let something slip." Ahead lay the

outskirts of Carson City showing bright lights against a purple sky fading rapidly to black. "Let's find a place to eat."

"At a time like this? I couldn't possibly eat."

Helen had a filet mignon dinner, asking for apple pie à la mode for dessert. I was the one who brooded, smoking more than I chewed, looking for answers in my coffee cup. When Helen had finished her meal, she touched her napkin to her lips and looked longingly at the slot machine across the room.

"I wonder if I should try my luck tonight or wait until to-morrow?"

"First thing in the morning, we check out of our room and catch a flight to Las Vegas," I announced, thus reaching a decision.

"Why Las Vegas?"

"Winch isn't at the Triangle K or at his home in the mountains. Vegas is what's left. Besides, it's a likely spot to find Renee Lassiter and some of the other people involved."

"Can't we drive down?"

"It's four hundred miles. Flying is faster."

"That's a good omen," Helen decided. "I might have played out my string in Reno. Las Vegas is my lucky city."

15

From a pay phone at the Reno airport the next morning, I called Farlow Hudspeth at the sheriff's office. My ostensible purpose was simply to report my travel plans, but my real intention was to pump him for the results of the gas chromatograph analysis of Renee's cocaine. That was no problem. He was telling me as soon as I had identified myself that the test had been positive—it had been laced with arsenic.

"I've got an appointment with the prosecutor this afternoon," he finished. "There's likely to be a warrant issued for Mrs. Lassiter as a result of that meeting."

This being Saturday, I calculated, the earliest a warrant could be issued would be Monday. "What charge?"

"For sure we've got her for possession. Sale, which includes giving it away, is another possibility. Righteous charges, but what they amount to is something to hold her on. What I'm really hoping for is a charge of homicide—manslaughter at least."

"Chancy," I judged. "You have nothing at all to show she introduced the arsenic."

"Let's see what the prosecutor says. Meanwhile, you run across her in Vegas or anywhere else, you let me know, hear?"

"Of course." No promise of how much later was either stated or implied.

"Warning a wanted felon of impending legal action is a crime in these parts. I mention that in case you have any idea of inducing her to flee."

That kind of law could be invoked only after charges were on file, but I wasn't about to admit I knew that. "Right. My plane is ready to leave now."

The commuter flight went southeast to Las Vegas on a trajectory like an arrow's. Well before noon, Helen and I debarked at the Las Vegas airport. Minutes later I had another rental car, a Mercury this time arranged in advance, tooling toward Las Vegas Boulevard South, the Strip. We passed some names I recognized, arriving at the Caravan between Caesars Palace and the Dunes, opposite the MGM Grand.

Helen entered the hotel lobby, looking into the action in the casino. I spotted the president of the Randolph Scott fan club, Clint Pettibone, about his security duties and was recognized by him in return. I knew that because he made for the nearest house phone. I went to the registration desk, where a clerk started giving me a line about the impossibility of getting a room for two on a weekend without a reservation. As I was about to give up, I saw Otis T. Bremmel approaching.

"We've had a cancellation. Give Mr. Disbro and his lady twelve-twelve." Bremmel turned his opaque glasses my way, smiling. "Always glad to be of service to friends from my hometown. Is this visit business or pleasure?"

"Business for me, pleasure for her." I introduced Helen to Bremmel, who bowed over her hand in a manner that was strangely Continental for a kid from Cleveland raised under the tutelage of Shondor Birns. I asked, "Is Mrs. Lassiter still here?"

"Oh yes. I'm sure you'll find her at our tables this evening. Her luck has not improved any."

"Her credit rating has jumped since she became heir to the Lastec fortune."

Bremmel let a smile like the AB line in a geometry book stretch across his face. "Is she the business you spoke of?"

126

"Partly. I really wanted to see Harry Winch. Is he still betting against her?"

"Off and on." Bremmel didn't seem as concerned about Winch's habits as he had four days ago. "He seems to have spent some time traveling."

"You told me you once had him followed to his motel. Where would that be?"

"Downtown." He inclined his head to the north. "It's called the Bunkhouse. Hardly competition for us." He bowed again to Helen. "You are being comped here, so our prices are even better."

"Comped?" Helen asked when we were in the elevator after registering.

I explained it to her. "It happens to all you high rollers. Would I be original in observing that knowing people in the right places is more important than any number of academic degrees?"

Tipping the bellhop was my only excuse for going up to Room 1212. Helen was undecided between the pool and the gaming room. She said she would stay here until she made up her mind. I claimed the rental car again for a trip downtown.

BUNKHOUSE INN
Rooms $17 Up
Efficiencies

The motel was on the main highway in a section of town the travel brochures don't advertise, a place of losers in the big roll. Pawnshops and secondhand stores and people more interested in the sidewalk than the sights of Gamblers' Paradise. The dirty little secret of Las Vegas is that this part of town is essential to the economy of the Strip. For there to be winners, there have to be losers. For the losers to survive, there has to be a place to pawn the valuables, sell the bedroom suite, sell the car, find shelter for the night while waiting for the next natural to come up.

There are more losers than winners.

I parked among the guest spaces at the motel and entered

the office where a man who looked as if he should have been riding with Pancho Villa told me Harry Winch occupied number 10. It turned out to be off the second-floor balcony, one of the efficiencies. I knocked and waited, knocked and waited again. After the third try, I went back to the office to complain.

"He's not there."

"Ees not calabooso. He can leave if he want." The clerk's face held three days' worth of beard stubble that could not conceal the knife scar under his right eye. His Hawaiian shirt was open, exposing an undershirt going gray, with a stain of red sauce on it.

I let him see what a twenty-dollar bill looks like. He waved a fan with a scene of Jesus preaching by the shores of the Sea of Galilee and an advertisement for a funeral home. "I'd like to see inside."

"Can't be done."

I started the twenty back to my pocket.

"Maybe I get careless. Leave key out." He reached into a pigeon hole for 10 and removed the key.

I laid the twenty on the counter. He dropped the key beside it, turned and went through a curtained doorway behind the counter. The twenty was gone. I picked up the key and let myself into Winch's apartment.

It was called that because it had a nook for a kitchenette and a table at which two people could sit. The bed could have been folded into a couch, but it was still open and unmade. Otherwise, the place was another motel room. I went through it in a hurry, checking the drawers and the closet. His clothes were the most interesting part. Each change was a costume that would alter his appearance—cowboy, businessman, vacationer—the way it had varied in the series of photographs Bremmel had shown me back in Cleveland. The drawers held underwear and socks that would have gone with any costume. On the floor in the closet niche was a suitcase that had an airline destination tag still attached to the handle: Cleveland.

The tiny refrigerator in the kitchenette held a six-pack of beer (two cans missing), three kinds of sandwich meat, a loaf of bread half gone, mustard, relish, and margarine bars. There was a package of hot dogs in the freezer. On the counter of the two-burner stove was a jar of instant Sanka. He watched his caffeine and cholesterol intake and the ashtrays were empty.

The bathroom told me he had taken Victor Kiam up on his challenge, brushed with Crest, slapped on Aqua Velva, and cured his hangovers with Advil. None of which I found particularly significant. I went back to the dresser in the main room where I found the nearest thing to a treasure.

Jammed into the space between the mirror and the frame along the right edge were five pawn tickets. They had come from Abe's Loans with an address down the street. I plucked them out one by one and, leaving my car where it was, walked to the pawnshop.

Abe was behind the counter in a cage similar to the one that protected Gladys and Rolf back at my office in Cleveland. Outside the cage, the shelves held the litter of every pawnshop in the world—guitars, horns, cameras, stereo equipment, radios. Helen would probably have had an idea on all that, something to do with the age of technology turning in its toys when hard times came. I passed on that now, intent on my business. I shoved the five tickets through the cage opening.

"Already?" Abe was looking at the dates on them. "These came in only Thursday."

"I don't want to redeem them. I only want to look at the items."

Abe looked up from the tickets to study my face. One eye, his left, had a cast over it that caused his lid to droop. The other eye seemed to be open extra wide to do double duty. "You're not a cop."

"Private." I showed him a card.

"From Cleveland? Quite a distance. Is there something wrong with the stuff?"

"I'll know that when I see it." I showed him the engraver's version of Andrew Jackson's portrait. The way I was throwing twenties around would have bothered my conscience if it hadn't been Lassiter's money. "Old Hickory is requesting it."

Abe looked at the bill and then at me. He put the bill in his vest pocket, coming to a decision. He got out a ledger that listed the pawn ticket numbers in order. "Furs and jewelry."

"That doesn't help much."

He pressed a buzzer that unlocked a door in his cage. I stepped through and followed him to a back storeroom I assumed was the place he kept recent items until the owner failed to redeem them and they could go on sale. It made me think of the property room in a police department. Abe was a small man with a pronounced hump in his back. He carried his ledger with him, using it as a guide to the location of each item. The furs were on a coatrack. One was a stole, the other a full-length coat. Both had labels from Cleveland stores.

"Real mink," Abe assured me as he went to an old Diebold safe and worked the combination. He took out a black velvet box a little smaller than a cigar box. He opened the lid and showed me a pearl necklace. "Real pearls."

Next he removed a manila envelope and poured its contents onto the top of the safe. A cameo brooch. A diamond bracelet like a man's expansion watch band. A lady's Cartier watch. A gold pin with initials RL studded with varied-colored jewels.

"Real diamonds?" I asked.

"And other gems. All very good." Abe scooped them up and put them away, uneasy with them lying in the open. "Are they hot?"

"Not that I know of. How much is it all worth?"

"I allowed twenty thousand, but the actual value is maybe five times that."

"Who pawned them?"

Abe looked at the name on the ledger. "Homer Tracey."

That was a jolt. "What did he look like?"

"Around thirty." Abe studied me. "Not quite as tall as you. A little heavier. His mustache was dark where yours is light."

It sure hadn't been Homer Tracey. It might have been Harry Winch. "I'm not sure what's going down here. Best advice I can give is not to sell these things for the next couple weeks. I suspect they might be part of an estate."

"Then they might be stolen after all."

"Not exactly stolen. 'Misappropriated before the estate is settled' might be the words to describe it. I'm not even sure of that."

Abe was no stranger to good deals going sour. He locked everything back in place and showed me out of his storeroom. On the street again, I felt the desert heat pressing down on me, letting me know my corduroy jacket was not really required. I gave myself an IOU for a dip in the pool when I got back to the Caravan. Now I was headed for the Bunkhouse to replace the pawn tickets in Winch's mirror.

I climbed to the balcony and unlocked Winch's door. As soon as I had stepped across the threshold, I knew I had made a mistake in not knocking. A man was already in the room, looking a little surprised at my entrance. He had just been reaching for the knob of the television set, and he had a can of beer in his hand. He wore a tan leisure suit with a dark blue shirt open halfway to his navel. He was a little older, a little shorter, and a little heavier than I am, with a darker mustache.

"What the hell are you doing here?" I demanded in an authoritative voice.

"I live here." Harry Winch put down his can of beer. "I don't recall having a roommate."

I made a show of looking at the key in my hand. "I guess there's been a mistake." I started to back out.

Winch reached under his coat and came out with a Walther automatic. "Close the door," he said evenly, keeping the muzzle trained on my shirt. "Then put your hands up. That way I won't have to shoot you."

16

I shut the door and put up my hands, thus avoiding some painful bullet wounds.

"Turn around," Winch told me. "On your knees. Hands behind your head. Lean your forehead on the door."

"Is this some kind of yoga exercise?" But I did what he told me. When I was in position, Winch's hand gave me a thorough pat down, all the way to my socks. It occurred to me that the position I was in would have been appropriate to receiving a head wound similar to Gruznik's.

Finished with the frisk, Winch backed off. "Stay on your knees but turn around and face me."

I managed it, knowing what Jose Ferrer must have felt like playing Toulouse-Lautrec.

"Toss the key up on the bed." When it landed, Winch picked it up and examined it before he laid it on the dresser. "Slow and easy, get out some ID and throw it on the bed."

I gave him my identification case with my P.I. card. Winch looked puzzled when he first read it but soon the answer came to him. "Oh yeah. The one Lassiter hired." He looked up at me. "What are you doing out here?"

"Investigating."

"Lassiter is dead."

"His money lives on. Besides, I'm having a good time on his expense account."

Winch tossed my ID back to me and looked around his own room. His eyes came to his dresser mirror and stopped there, then returned to me. "Where are they?"

"My coat pocket."

"Put them back."

I took the pawn tickets out, showing them to him, and got onto my feet to lay them on his dresser. Winch kept the gun on me from across the room. I helped myself to a seat on the foot of his bed.

"So now you know I pawned Renee's valuables." He sat in a chair in a remote corner by the kitchenette and picked up his beer. "It doesn't matter. I wasn't trying to hide it."

"That's why you used the name Homer Tracey."

"It was something that popped into my head. I knew his wife from the dude ranch."

"Couldn't your own name pop into your head?" I asked.

"Habit. Never use your real name unless you have to." He sipped his beer.

"Why did you steal Renee's furs and jewels?"

Winch laughed, genuinely amused. "That's a good one, coming from you. In the first place, they weren't stolen. If they had been, though, you would have been an accomplice."

"Me?"

He nodded in verification, still smiling. "You're the one who gave Renee a ride to the hotel the night Lassiter was murdered, aren't you? You helped her carry her suitcases out, didn't you? What the fuck do you think was inside those suitcases?"

"Oh." I let Winch see I was reaching for a cigarette and used the time it took me to light it to do some figuring. "She packed her most valuable possessions and handed them over to you? Why?"

"She was short on ready cash. With her husband dead and the estate being tied up, it was the quickest way she saw at the time to raise some money. It might not have been the smartest move on earth, but her thinking isn't always crystal clear."

"She didn't need to do it. Bremmel was extending her credit."

"Maybe he was." Winch tapped his chest with the beer can while he kept the muzzle of his automatic pointed at me. "I wasn't."

"Why did she owe you money?"

"Services rendered." Winch slaked his beer and crushed the can in his hand. "While I was on the Triangle K, I helped her with an onerous task."

"Which was?"

"Slightly illegal." Winch regarded me with a doubtful eye. "Exactly where do you stand in all this with Lassiter gone?"

It was a question I hadn't settled in my own mind. "He hired me to watch out for his wife's welfare. I suppose you could say she inherited my loyalty along with the mansion in Bratenahl."

"Suppose I would tell you that poking around this mess will only get her in deep shit. Will you butt out?"

"Given enough details, I might."

Winch waved the Walther he still held steadily in his hand. "Once I tell you, there's no going back. I don't do hard time for any cunt, nor any rent-a-cop that wants to play games. Let what I tell you out of this room, I waste you. Understood?"

"Understood."

"The only reason I'm willing to talk is because you will keep at it if I don't. Anyway, you can't use this against me."

I inhaled smoke and let him rant through the preliminaries. Soon he would talk himself into telling me what I wanted to know.

"I helped Renee get rid of Shana Tracey's body," he said in a rush. Once that was out, he was over the worst part.

"Why did Renee kill her?" I asked.

"Renee didn't kill her. The worst thing she did was supply Shana with some coke. It killed Shana like it's killed others. Maybe there's a charge in that, but it's not murder. Renee wanted to avoid that hassle, so she came to me for help. That's the whole thing. Try to make any more out of it, you might send me over, but you'll be making ten times the trouble for her."

"Where did this happen?"

"On the Triangle K in Renee's room. Shana snorted the coke in there and keeled over."

Except for the arsenic in the cocaine, it could have been that simple. "Tell me about the rest of it."

"Nothing much to tell. I put Shana's body in her car and drove out into the wilds. Renee followed in my car. I drove to an access road and up that until it ran out, and then I carried Shana's body as far as I could. That's where I dumped her in a ravine. With any kind of luck, it wouldn't have been found for months, years even. It was my bad luck they found it as soon as they did. After the body had been dumped, I went back to the car where Renee was waiting for me."

"This was at night?"

"Early morning, if you want to get technical. It was coming up on dawn by the time we got back to the ranch. Renee packed her things, and I drove her to the airport, where she caught the flight to Vegas. Next day I told Viola I was quitting, and then I left and drove down here."

"And started gambling against Renee."

"It was what we worked out. I didn't do all this out of the goodness of my heart. Renee had lots of credit but not much cash. Anyway, I didn't want her paying me directly in case it should come up later. Once she had established credit, she could gamble at the tables in the Caravan, which is where I sent her because I knew the place. The way she gambles, I was sure she would lose. I made it a point to play at her table each day and bet against her. Most of the time it worked out, and I came out ahead. When she had a run of luck, she turned the winnings over to me. Either way, I couldn't lose."

At last I had an explanation of the scam they had been working. "How long was this supposed to last?"

"It was kind of open-ended. I figured it might go on for a month."

"Why did she make the trip back to Cleveland?"

"Ask Bremmel. It was his doing." Winch shifted in his chair, without moving his gun hand. "You want my opinion, Bremmel wanted to ensure Renee's credit. He had her with him in case Lassiter refused to pay. Like ransom."

But Bremmel had known Renee's credit was good a day before her plane left Las Vegas. "None of this could have affected Lassiter's murder?"

"That was a whole 'nother thing. Renee tells me the police pinned it on the chauffeur."

"Maybe that's because the police didn't know you were in Cleveland at the time."

Winch's lounge lizard eyes opened up at that, the effect I had been after.

"Your suitcase has a Cleveland tag on it," I explained. "Want me to start checking airlines?"

"I flew to Cleveland," he said, "about three hours ahead of Renee. She was being held in her room like a prisoner on Monday. Bremmel's ape, Fred, was guarding her door. When he told her to pack a trip to Cleveland, she called me here. I told her I would head for Cleveland and stay at the Bond Court Hotel because that's the name of the hotel she gave me. Too bad you took her to a different hotel. I guess it would have been too convenient for you to bring her right to me."

"Yeah. I did enough carrying her suitcases for her. She never got in contact with you?"

"Sure she did. At her house before the police came, she went upstairs, remember? She called me then. I told her to pack the valuables and bring them with her."

Now the truth emerged. Bringing the furs and jewelry had been Winch's idea. "One problem you have in your story—it puts you in Cleveland in time to kill Lassiter."

"So what? I didn't do it. For one thing, I stayed in the hotel waiting to hear from Renee. For another, I'd have no reason for killing Lassiter."

"It still would be a good idea to protect your flanks. Now that the cops don't have Gruznik anymore, they might come looking for you."

Winch leaned forward in his chair, pushing the Walther ahead of him. I knew with certainty at that instant he could pull the trigger anytime. "You get around. When did you find him?"

"Sunset yesterday."

"I didn't do it," Winch told me, and relaxed a little. I let my heels touch the floor again. "I found him a couple hours ahead of you. Someone left his body in my yard. The Mercedes was parked there, too."

"So you were at Tahoe yesterday?"

"What of it? I went up there to take care of my business. When I stopped by my house, there was the Mercedes and there was his body in my yard. I put the body in the car and drove it off into the woods."

"You're starting to make a habit of moving other people's bodies."

"I haven't heard about Gruznik being found on the news," Winch mused. "Didn't you call the cops?"

"I couldn't find a phone."

"Well." Winch studied me some more.

"That Walther could be the piece that killed him."

"It isn't." He dropped the magazine out, jacked the shell out of the chamber and tossed me the remains. "See for yourself."

I caught the pistol and pulled down on the trigger guard, releasing the slide so it could move forward off the frame. The .380 barrel, mounted on the frame, was clean. I reassembled the piece and gave it back. "It's been cleaned."

"You're going to fault me for taking care of my weapons?"

"What was Gruznik doing at your place anyway?"

"Who knows? The way I figure it, my place has been standing vacant for so long, someone might have picked it for a secluded meeting place. They lured Gruznik up there and shot him and left the body for me to find." He laid the pistol and the magazine down separately, maybe a sign he trusted me.

"I don't like the idea that Gruznik committed murder and then drove across the whole damned country to die on your doorstep."

"If you're asking my opinion, I don't approve of it either. When you get back to Cleveland, ask Duane Lagrasso. Gruznik was his man."

"For sure?"

"When I was dealing at the Caravan, Lagrasso came out on business trips. Gruznik was his bodyguard."

The connections among the people in this case were growing like the arrows on a flowchart, getting so numerous they looked like cobwebs. "I'll have to look into that."

When I started for the door, Winch stopped me to give me the extra room key, the one I had obtained from the desk clerk. "Return that to Luis on your way out. Let on like nothing happened."

I bounced the key on my palm and then exited with a two-finger salute to Winch.

17

The swim I had promised myself seemed like a better idea than ever when I returned to the Caravan. Not all the sweating I had done that afternoon had been caused by the hot weather. Helen was not in room 1212. I changed to a pair of swim trunks and thought of one more chore to be done before I indulged in recreation. I got an outside line and called Cleveland information to ask for the number of North Coast Investments.

A recording told me they would be open for business again Monday morning. My years in police work and the detective trade have pretty well wiped out my concept of weekends and holidays, putting me just far enough out of sync to regard them as a nuisance because they mean most places are closed when you need them. A five-day work cycle—like a nine-to-five work-day—is a concept I have never adapted to. My idea has always been you do the work when it needs doing and quit when it's done even if it means going to bed when the rest of the world is getting up. Among other things, reasoning like that explains why I never settled into a sensible line of work.

I called 216 information again to see if Audrey Carnahan's

number was listed. The best they could do was A. Carnahan with a number and an address that put her in Condominium Country along I-271. I tried the number and got her on the fifth ring.

"Oh, it's you," she said when I had identified myself. From an object of disgust, I had climbed the social ladder to indifference.

"A little problem," I told her. "Would you know the name of the insurance company Lassiter used for his wife's valuables?"

"Not offhand. Why would you want to know that?"

"I was hoping he might have photographs of the furs and jewelry on file." I explained that items I suspected of being Renee's had turned up in a Las Vegas pawnshop.

"Try describing them," she invited. "I might recognize something."

I went through them as best I could. The mink coat and stole. The pin with the RL initials. The diamond bracelet. The cameo brooch.

"That one?" Audrey exploded angrily. "It has a profile of a nineteenth-century woman with upswept hair?"

"Sounds right."

"That bitch! I didn't think even Renee was capable of such a mercenary trick! That was an heirloom handed down through the Lassiter family. She has no right to dispose of it."

"You're sure about that?"

"Boyd showed it to me once and explained its history."

I didn't ask how she had come to be in Lassiter's bedroom, going over his heirlooms. "All is not lost. None of the items I described are going to be sold. Find the name of his insurance company first thing Monday and call it in to my secretary. I'll get in touch with them and find out what they want done. There might even be a reward."

"I'm not interested in any reward."

"I am." I made sure she had my office number and hung up.

I scrawled Helen a note on hotel stationery saying I had gone to the pool, whither I went. As soon as I had found a place to lay my robe and towel, I ran to the edge of the pool at the five-foot level, put my head down, and dived in. I let my momentum skim me under the water's surface, emerging halfway across the pool. Three long strokes took me to the opposite side. I grasped the edge of the pool and pulled myself out of the water into a sitting position on the cement, all in one motion. Mastering that little trick had taken me most of the summer after my sophomore year in high school. How I had hated guys who did that until I joined their ranks.

Along the fence on that side of the pool was a line of chaise longues populated by foxes in minimalist bikinis. They didn't cheer me or hold up cards with numbers on them, but I knew that behind their sunglasses they were admiring my outstanding example of the male form. I knew they were. I dived back into the pool and floated on my back. When I had accustomed myself to the water, my first opportunity to swim since last summer, I decided it was time to go to the diving boards.

I went off the low board twice, getting the feel again, before I turned to the three-meter tower. My first effort was a simple swan dive, but it contained all the elements that make diving the poetic experience it always has been for me. The spring off the board into midair. The instant of pause at the apex, when you seem to have broken free of earth's restrictions. Then the plummeting down, water rushing up, as gravity reasserts its power. Finally, knifing into the water cleanly with virtually no sense of impact when the form is good. I surfaced, climbed out of the pool and headed for the board again. More sunglasses than ever—all worn by the foxes in the bikinis—were turned my way as I passed by them.

I dived a few more times—a jackknife, a half gainer, a somersault when I wrapped my arms around my knees like a trapeze artist. I was starting to wear down. The body that had served me so well at eighteen was beginning to fail me now. While I could still hack it, I walked slowly out on to the end of the board where I did a handstand. Poised there, I launched myself off head-down and sliced into the water.

Are there any bikinis I haven't impressed?

When I came up from the deep-end ladder, I spotted one just arriving. The swimsuit was an aqua flower pattern, although it didn't contain enough material to portray a whole bouquet. The body to which it was tentatively attached was thin, maybe too thin. Her shoulders were pointed and her shoulder blades stood out prominently. None of which kept her from filling the suit the way it was designed to be filled, an achievement for her thirty-odd years. She was Renee Lassiter.

She settled onto a vacant chaise, putting her things on a tin table at its side. When she had settled in, I toweled my hair and myself, meandering her way. Standing above her, I admired her flat stomach devoid of a wrinkle. A few tantalizing tendrils of pubic hair escaped the bottom of her suit at the crotch.

"Good to see you again, Mrs. Lassiter."

She looked over the top of her sunglasses, seeing only as high as my navel and the hair matted around it. "Get lost."

"I'm not trying to hit on you," I promised. "We really have met before, in Cleveland."

This time she really looked at me, imagining me with clothes. "You're the detective Boyd hired, the one who tried to rescue me from the clutches of evil men." She smiled to show she was being ironic. "Did I ever thank you properly?"

"You left town too fast."

She moved her legs, allowing me room to sit on the flat portion of the chaise. "Are you here on a vacation?"

"Working. Still earning the money Boyd paid me."

"Is that necessary?" she asked. "I'm not going to complain if you take it and run."

"I'm supposed to be protecting your interests, Renee. Right now I'm worried about your welfare because you're here instead of in Cleveland."

She smiled again. "Because you're afraid I'll gamble my money away?"

"Because you're not here willingly. These guys have a hold on you, though I'm not sure what it is. Bremmel is using it, but the source of his power seems to be Duane Lagrasso. You're welcome to tell me about it any time. I'm on your side."

She waited too long, not denying it and not laughing in my face. "You have a wild imagination."

Her Marlboros were lying on the table beside her, with a Bic lighter. "Do you mind?" I lit one and inhaled. "Sure tastes good. It seems like I can't recall a time when I didn't smoke."

"I know what you mean." She shifted in her seat so that her thigh rubbed against mine. It was hard to think the touch was accidental.

I inhaled again and said, "Whatever the hold they have on you, it has nothing to do with Shana's death at the Triangle K. It goes back further than that."

She whipped off her sunglasses and stared at me with her hazel eyes. "What—" She couldn't think of a question to go with the word.

"I talked to Harry Winch an hour ago."

"Then—" She looked around to make sure no one was within earshot. Even so, she kept her voice down. "What do you want?"

"Straight answers."

"I've given you all I can."

"You haven't given me diddly squat. I understand your reluctance to trust me, but soon you have to start. You had better get out of Nevada by Monday because the authorities around Reno are going to have a warrant out for your arrest by then. Tell Bremmel about that. Explain to him you have to leave the state. If they arrest you, they could bring your case before the grand jury. The charge could be as serious as murder."

She shook her head. "They couldn't do that. At worst, Shana's death was an accident. I didn't try to kill her."

"You gave her cocaine that turns out to have been laced with arsenic." I gave her time to let that bit of information sink in. "Where did it come from?"

"Are you some kind of narc?" There was a quality in her voice that made the question more a challenge to a contest she might enjoy.

"It's the last thing I would ever be. Did you get the coke from Steve Stockman?"

"You're wasting your breath. It's a question I'd never answer."

"Did Audrey Carnahan bring it to you when she visited the Triangle K?"

"Same as before."

"Did your husband ever have any access to it?"

"I'm leaving." Renee stood up, but I got hold of her arm and pulled her back down.

"You'll hear me out on this one," I promised her. "If you won't give me an answer, you'll hear what I've doped out. The person who supplied you with that poisoned cocaine was trying to kill you. I think that person was your husband. Lassiter let you come to Reno for your divorce, but he gave you the going-away present. He knew that sooner or later you'd use it, so he sat back and waited for the call informing him he was a widower. Only it didn't come. Instead, he got word you were alive and well in Vegas. He hired me because he wanted to find out what went wrong, not knowing that Shana Tracey had taken the fatal dose and you had dumped her body."

"I don't believe you. Boyd wouldn't—"

"Yes, he would. He had come into a lot of money and he wasn't going to risk losing part of it in a divorce settlement. Now tell me I'm wrong. Tell me he never had a chance to poison your coke."

"So there you are."

The voice startled me almost as much as it did Renee. Helen had come up while we were so intently engaged. She, too, wore a bikini to good advantage. Seeing Helen without clothes was hardly a unique experience for me, but seeing her like this was a treat I had forgotten during the last six months. Total nudity stirs me as much as the next guy but near nudity, with crucial parts barely concealed, does things to my testosterone that are hard to ignore. It sent a shock wave of lust mingled with pride coursing through my bloodstream. No more troubled by cellulite than Renee was, Helen managed to maintain her weight without Renee's near-anorexic thinness. Instead of being sharp and angular, Helen was nicely rounded where it counted.

"Am I interrupting something?" Helen asked.

"Not a thing." I let go of Renee's arm and stood up to intro-

duce the girls. They eyed one another, the way women will, like
two gunslingers meeting on the dusty street of a cow town.

Helen recovered from her surprise in time to make some appropriate noises. "It was a shame about your husband's death. I
knew him slightly from conferences between our colleges."

Renee seemed stumped for an appropriate reply. She made
a show of looking at her watch. "I have to be going." I couldn't
imagine her not having a social calendar filled with appointments.

When Renee had vacated the chaise longue, Helen moved in.
She settled down with suntan lotion and sunglasses.

"The water is fine," I pointed out.

"I think I'll just sit here and absorb the rays."

Going to a swimming pool to sit on the sidelines is like going
to a ball game to watch the hot dogs cook. Sunbathing is a nonac-
tivity I have always classified with sitting in bars or going fishing.
I tried a few minutes of it. "How is your gambling going?"

"Up and down," she admitted. "I was ahead a little and then
I started losing. I'm down now by about four hundred dollars."

"Well, you're still three hundred ahead."

"I'm taking a break now. When I go back later, my luck will
turn. I'm due."

I stayed on land another five minutes, the absolute limit of my
patience. "Time to go back in the water," I said, standing up.

"I'll stay here. It feels so good with the sun beating down."

I picked up Helen and started carrying her toward the deep
end of the pool.

"Gil, what do you think you're doing? Put me down this instant! Gil, people are watching. Come on, now. Enough. You
wouldn't dare! Gil!"

She hit the water with a splash Shamu would have admired.
When she broke the surface, treading, she showed me a look of
disapproval before she struck out for the far side with a scissors
kick. I dived in after her and swam along on a sidestroke. We
kept going like that, like a scene from an Esther Williams movie.
When we tired of that, we went back to 1212 and made love.

18

We went downstairs much later for dinner. The featured act in the main lounge was a comic whose concept of humor was saying "fuck" three times each sentence. Helen was willing to pass on that for a simple dinner before she went to the tables. After we had eaten, while we were dawdling over cigarettes and coffee, the waiter informed me our check had been comped. I left him another of Lassiter's twenties.

Helen had graduated from slot machines to roulette and now was shooting craps. She ignored my advice that blackjack at least allowed a fighting chance (too slow for her taste) and went to the very crap table where Renee had been photographed. Helen started rolling and losing. I was seriously considering adopting Winch's strategy of betting against her to save something from her losses when I sensed an object beside me roughly the size of a lamppost. It was Clint Pettibone observing the play as if it were a Randolph Scott movie.

Without taking his eyes off the action, he said, "Mr. Bremmel wishes to talk to you." His Indian features impassive, Clint turned and walked away.

After motioning to Helen, I followed. He led me through the lobby on to a mezzanine that led to banquet rooms. A hall off that led to a corridor of offices for the staff. We entered one that was not marked. The spacious room beyond was probably an office because it had a desk at one end. More prominent was a conference table and an area set up like a corner of a hotel lobby. Otis T. Bremmel was there, on a couch, scowling over a series of accounting sheets spread over the cocktail table in front of him. He pointed his cigar at a chair opposite his seat. "Be right with you."

I went to my designated chair. When I had settled into it, I saw Bremmel had not been alone. Fred—the thug who looked like a Teamsters official, who had accompanied Renee from the airport—was standing by a side bar around a corner that had hidden him from sight when I first entered. Clint closed the door, staying inside.

"Want something to drink?" Fred asked me.

I passed. Bremmel was working a pocket calculator, glancing at the accounting sheets, punching numbers from them onto the tiny screen. He entered the last figure and looked at the total, not finding a lot of satisfaction with the result. He accepted it, though, and closed the cover on the calculator. He moved all the papers into one pile and stacked them at the end of the table. Done, he removed his thick glasses and rubbed his eyes.

"Fuckin' work's never done." He looked up at a point four feet to my left. It was the first time I had seen his eyes without the glasses, brown and wide open in an effort to see. "Mrs. Lassiter tells me you talked to her earlier."

"So I did."

He turned his head slightly, honing in on my voice. "You warned her there might be a warrant on her early next week. I called some people in Reno. Deputy sheriff up there named Hudspeth signed a complaint today and left it at the judge's office. I got hold of the judge, who will have to sign it first thing Monday. It looks like your information was good."

"What will the charge be?"

"Trafficking in cocaine." Bremmel put his glasses back on,

147

seeing me for the first time but shielding his eyes from my sight. "It appears to be a holding charge until they can take the case before the grand jury, hoping for an indictment on something much more serious. We—Mrs. Lassiter, at least—owes you a debt of gratitude for warning her. The first order of business will be getting her out of Nevada before an arrest can occur."

"She can't run forever," I pointed out.

"Time works in our favor. The police can't act until the judge signs the warrant, which gives us the weekend to get her out of Nevada's clutches. Hudspeth can't stop her from leaving until the warrant is issued."

"There's such a thing as extradition."

"Extradition proceedings can be delayed a long time. An hour ago, we put her on a commuter flight to Denver, where she can make connections for Cleveland. A judge we know back there can be very technical in extradition matters. If it drags out long enough, Nevada might lose interest."

"Or it might not."

Bremmel allowed himself a tight smile. "The police have such a naïve faith that the law will be followed. At least they proceed on that assumption. They forget that the law is there to be manipulated to the advantage of anyone who can pay for it."

"In which case she would lose her opportunity to prove guilt or innocence." I shook out a cigarette and rolled it in my fingers.

"Small loss. Defending yourself in court can be tedious and draining, emotionally and financially. Why go through a trial if it's not necessary?"

"She happens to be innocent," I said, "the victim of a murder attempt by her late husband."

Bremmel puffed hard on his cigar, trying to get it going after ignoring it too long. "Mrs. Lassiter told me about your theory. Most interesting. It does seem, though, that there would be little point in smearing Mr. Lassiter now that he's dead."

Letting that remark pass, I pushed the cigarette into my face and lit it. "You seem to have a lot of interest in what happens to Renee. Why?"

"Good customer."

I shook my head. "You're into something deeper than that."

Bremmel allowed himself a small smile. "Really, Disbro, your fantasies are so good I can hardly wait to hear what it is you imagine is going on."

"Lastec, Incorporated," I said, "at this moment has the auto industry by the balls. When the new emissions standards go into effect, no one will be able to put a car on an American highway without the Lastec gasket. At least not until someone comes up with something better. Control Mrs. Lassiter, and you control the company."

"Hmm." Bremmel looked at Clint. He looked at Fred. He looked at his cigar. "How would we do that?"

"My first thought was the obvious one. Keep her gambling, keep her losing. When she gets far enough behind, she has to put up her share of stock in the company. When she loses that, you're in the auto supply business."

"Would that it were that easy," he said almost wistfully.

"I told you it was only my first thought. Now I realize it isn't that simple. Duane Lagrasso knows her from some time back. Whatever he knows makes her your prisoner. That's why you brought her to Cleveland, to see Lagrasso in person so he could whip her into line. Before that she owed you a little money which she would have had no problem paying. After that session in Cleveland, she's been ready to jump whenever you crack the whip. A few words from you and she boards a plane to fly to wherever you want her to be."

"Even if all that happened to be true, you're still forgetting the most important factor," Bremmel told me. "Lastec is a corporation with a board of directors, with financial advisers, with layers of management to go through before any decision is made. Not many of them are likely to be swayed by a woman's whim, even if she is the widow of the founder."

"There are ways around it. How much of an interest does Renee hold? More than thirty percent, I'd bet. Suppose Leisure Pursuits launched a takeover bid on Lastec. You would have a lot of mob money backing you, more than shows on the books. You might be successful but more likely, Lastec would buy you off by offering a share of the stock. Then your block added to Renee's block might put you over the top. Or you could dicker with General Motors or any other company that might be tired of outsourcing. They would be thrilled to get a piece of Lastec. There are all kinds of possibilities. Big risks and big stakes. You really don't need the whole shooting match. A piece of the action will do for a start."

"My, my," Bremmel said, but the pain on his face told me my ideas were hitting close. "You do go on."

I took a final drag off my cigarette and crushed it out. "Want to hear a better one? What happens to Renee once she has served her purpose? The time comes when it would be more expedient for her to die, leaving Leisure Pursuits her interest in Lastec. Six months down the road, maybe."

Clint took a step away from the door and stood spread-legged, ready to be ordered into action. Bremmel held his hand out palm-up and looked at me. "You certainly spin an interesting yarn. Someone with your imagination deserves a reward."

"I'll settle on one straight answer. What do you have on Renee Lassiter?"

"Imagination like yours and persistence can make a bad combination. It can lead to following a paranoid fantasy beyond all hope."

"So tell me what you have on her."

Bremmel knocked ash off his cigar. "A bright man like you deserves to advance in the world. How would you like to be head of your own agency? You could employ several operatives, even an entire force of uniformed personnel. I have contacts with many companies in need of security."

"Jesus, you give subtlety a new name. You don't have to bribe me like that. Tell me what Renee did. She must have killed somebody. It's the only thing I can think of serious enough to give you a hold like you've got."

"How would you like," Bremmel said evenly, "to be a skeleton bleached under the desert sun?"

"Those are my choices? Either I turn into the next Allan Pinkerton or a corpse? One I'm not qualified for and the other I'm not ready for. I'll have to pass on them both."

"You are no longer welcome here," Bremmel informed me. "Please have the decency to leave the hotel as soon as you can arrange transportation home."

The ultimate punishment. He had taken away my privilege of being comped. I tried hard not to laugh. "Don't fret on it. I spotted a neat railroad trestle today that would be great to sleep under." I headed for the door where Clint blocked my path. "Out of my way, hombre. This room ain't big enough for the two of us."

He looked over my shoulder to get his signal from Bremmel and then stepped aside. Warily I walked past him and yanked the door open. Before I could step through it, all hell broke loose.

Now it's fairly easy to reconstruct what happened. At the time, it was a rush of pain, surprise, and humiliation without sense. When I had passed him, Clint drove a fist into my kidney that arched my back and raised me onto my toes. While I was in that position, he karate-chopped the back of my neck to send me headlong into the hall. Except I caught the door frame and got in my one good lick, a kick intended for Clint's gonads that got his navel instead. He went down on one knee, and I pivoted, swinging a punch for his face. By that time Fred had moved up to smash his fist into my cheekbone. I tumbled backward into the hall and landed on my keister.

"See what can happen to you?" Fred asked, and hauled me to my feet. He held one arm while Clint grasped the other. They pulled me back into the room, and one of them kicked the door shut behind me.

Bremmel stayed on the couch, contemplating me while he puffed on his cigar. "You are a difficult man to deal with. Difficult to bribe. Difficult to threaten." He puffed away, sorting through solutions to the problem. "How is your tolerance to pain?"

Clint took that for a cue to do something to my arm that pinched a nerve. I bit my lower lip and made no sound. That disappointed Clint so much he twisted something else. The sound that escaped my teeth was more a hiss than a gasp, and my eyes smarted. I went down on my knees, but the two goons held on to my arms.

"Ease up on him," Bremmel said. The tone of his voice was

not concerned with my welfare. He was looking on this from an economic standpoint. Sure they could have put me in ICU, but their point had been made without that much effort. Why break five bones if breaking one will make the same point? Why break any bones if you can get by wrenching an arm?

Somehow that careful calibration struck me as more terrifying than a thorough beating.

Clint relaxed his grip with a sigh of disappointment. My right arm flopped at my side, an appendage evolution had rendered obsolete.

"You macho types amuse me," Bremmel noted. "You put such store in covering up your feelings. That doesn't prove you are fearless. It simply shows you fear giving in more than you fear pain or injury or death."

"Hell, why didn't you tell me you wanted me to scream soprano?" I rubbed my arm, trying to get feeling into it again. Flexing my fingers was out of the question.

"Still, the macho pose seems to have the greatest attraction to the ladies," Bremmel observed. "Now take your companion, Mrs. Scagnetti. A lovely lady. What a shame if anything should spoil her looks."

He had punched a button this time. "You try that, you're dead. I'll kill you. Hear me?"

Bremmel took it with equanimity. Threats from a one-armed man on his knees have a way of seeming less dangerous.

"My, aren't we a strange group? Throwing threats around indiscriminately?" Bremmel nodded to Clint, who moved behind me. Something cold and metallic pressed against my temple. It was Clint's Blackhawk. "Remember this moment," Bremmel advised. "I will not tolerate your crazy allegations or your harassment."

There was nothing I could do. My right arm was still numb, and the muzzle was too close to dodge.

Clint put his piece away, and I stood up. This time there was no stopping me when I stepped out into the hall. Hurting in various places, I headed for the casino to locate Helen. She was not there. Managing to flex my arm now, I checked the coffee shop and the bar without success before I tried room 1212 where I found her already in bed. Good enough. I could use the rest myself. I stripped down to my shorts and got in beside her. I put my good arm around her and we nestled together like two pieces of a jigsaw puzzle. In a little while I drifted off to sleep.

It was one of the worst nights for sleeping I could remember, not because I was cringing from the threats or because the pain of the brief fight was so great, but because Helen was so restless. She flopped from one side to another, elbowing my ribs every time I was sliding down the deep end of a sleep curve. About the time I was ready to move to the couch for some peace, Helen got out of bed. A few seconds later I heard the snick of a lighter and the hiss of butane. I lay still awhile longer before I slit my eyes open to see the red glow of her cigarette by the window. She was sitting with her legs drawn up, her arms wrapped around her knees. She had been sleeping in an oversized T-shirt with the face of Charles Dickens on it.

I swung my feet over the side of the bed and turned on a weak light on the nightstand. Helen was still in the shadows. "What's wrong?" I asked.

"What do you think?" she countered.

The list of possible problems wasn't all that long. "Your paper on this Hardy guy isn't going well."

"It isn't going at all." She inhaled a puff. "That's not the problem."

"You lost the seven hundred dollars."

"Worse than that. I lost my own money, too."

"How much?"

"Five hundred dollars."

"Hell, that's no problem. I've got more than that in expense money. You're welcome to it."

"The amount isn't that important. It's the way I went about it. When I blew the seven hundred, I wrote out a check for the five hundred. When that was gone, I was on my way back to draw another thousand. Suddenly I realized what I was doing as if I were coming out of a dream. What happened to me?"

"You were bitten by the gambling bug." I yawned. "Now that we've settled that, let's go to sleep."

"You knew it was going to happen to me."

"I didn't know. I was afraid it might."

"I was caught in a downward spiral. On a conscious level I knew I was throwing my money away, but I couldn't stop doing it. I just knew the next roll of the dice would make my fortune."

"Compulsive behavior." I yawned again. "It's what makes alcoholics and dope addicts. Without it, this community would be desert sand."

"But me, Helen Scagnetti, B.A., M.A., Ph.D. I'm no slum kid shooting heroin. I should know better. I should exercise more control over my life."

"Sweetheart," I told her, "getting those sheepskins doesn't mean you turn in your membership card in the human race. Did you know we've been evicted from here?"

"What happened?" Her voice was a shriek I feared would wake the neighbors.

"I asked too many questions." I lay down again, but Helen wouldn't let me sleep until I told her what had transpired. "Maybe it's for the best," I concluded. "It will keep you from temptation at the crap tables."

A minute later, Helen turned out the light and crawled in beside me. A little later she was breathing heavily—not snoring because she insists she doesn't snore. It was my turn to lie abed with my eyes open. Time passed but sleep didn't come.

"Helen?"

"Uh."

"You awake?"

"Uh-huh."

"This Hardy guy writes books about people who are always crushed down by fate. Do I have that right?"

"He used to. He's dead now."

"Fate is like an outside force, right? When things are going well, something goes wrong and ruins the guy's life. Is that about it?"

Helen thrashed once more and came up on her elbow,

searching for my face in the dark. "It's not always a malevolent fate, but it usually works out that way. Fate is simply indifferent. Rain falls on the just and the unjust. Why do you ask questions like that at three o'clock in the morning?"

"I was thinking about what we said. Could it be that Hardy's characters suffer from compulsive behavior? They make the same mistakes over and over and blame it on fate?"

"I don't know. Could it be that Hardy had more insight into human nature than even he thought? He called it 'immutable fate,' but could it be something else?"

"Well, it's something for you to think about." Now that my idea had been relayed to her, I rolled over to sleep.

"Are you sure you're as ignorant about Hardy as you let on?"

"Maybe I looked at the Cliff Notes once."

When I woke up the next time, the sun was shining through the windows. Helen was sitting at the hotel desk jotting things down in her notebook.

19

Our plane landed at Cleveland Hopkins on Monday afternoon amidst a snowstorm typical of the squalls that blow off Lake Erie. Wind drove the flakes down diagonally, not a lot of them, swirling the snow across the runways like dust. Welcome back to the real world.

When Helen and I had collected our things at baggage claims, I hiked out to the parking deck to claim my car left there last week. We hadn't been able to get a flight out of Las Vegas on short notice on Sunday, meaning we'd had to spend an extra day on Bremmel's largess, a development that gave me no qualms whatsoever. Helen had stayed away from gambling without any trouble, absorbed in what I had said on the subject of this Hardy character. Her stumbling block was that she had left all her books on the subject back home, making it impossible for her to check references. We went out in search of a bookstore that would be open on Sunday and finally found one where Helen picked up a couple paperbacks. One of them was about a native coming home and the other one looked interesting because it concerned the mayor of Carmel, or some such place, but turned out not to be about Clint Eastwood at all.

With my car ransomed back, I circled around to pick up Helen and our bags at the terminal and drove us home. There had been lots of cold here but not much more snow. The main streets were about as bare as they would get before the next thaw, and the side streets were passable. We hadn't been in the house ten minutes until the phone rang. Helen took it and said to me, "For you."

When I had put the receiver to my ear and identified myself, the female voice said, "You told me to call you if I needed your help. I tried your office but you weren't there. Your secretary gave me this number. That's why I called."

"What's the problem, Renee?" I asked.

"It's out here. Can you come?"

"Where are you?"

"The house in Bratenahl."

Helen had already booted her word processor and was checking her bookshelves. When I hung up, she remarked, "Renee is the one in the aqua bikini."

"I was sort of hoping you would forget that."

"What does she want?"

"Her bra strap broke. She wants me to come tie the ends together."

"When will you be back—if at all? Should I leave you something to pop into the microwave?"

"One of the things I always admired about you is your total lack of jealousy. Work on your research, and I'll be back in time to take you to dinner."

The drive to Bratenahl was a straight shot down the Shoreway at a time of day when rush-hour traffic was still corralled in the downtown parking lots. Twenty minutes after I had left Helen, I pulled up to the house where this had all started. The courtyard had a light dusting of snow that covered the rivulets left by the last car wash Al Gruznik had ever given. For the third time in my life, I walked up to the front door.

Renee herself answered the knocker, dressed in slacks and a simple blouse to match her eyes. Her hair had been drawn back in a ponytail and she wore no makeup. "Thank God you're here."

She took me into the great hall past the doors to the library, heading for the staircase. A yellow plastic ribbon had been stretched across those doors. Red letters on the ribbon read: CRIME SCENE—DO NOT ENTER. Renee avoided looking at it as we passed.

"I can't stand this place," she told me. "I tried fixing up a couple rooms upstairs so I can stay there. I pretend it's an apartment in a big building. It's the only way I can survive."

"When did you get back?"

"Last night. It was Bremmel's idea to get me out of Nevada after I told him what you said. So it's your idea, too, in a way. I can't stay here long without the cops finding me to serve that warrant. Bremmel is going to find me a place in Miami."

"Otis T. is a real friend."

We had reached the upstairs hall by this time. Renee opened a door that led into what she had called her apartment, which was the master bedroom with a sitting room on one side and a bath on the other. Its windows, French doors leading to a balcony, looked out on to the rear, a view of the lake after an expanse of lawn with a boathouse and dock at the shoreline. I took it on faith that Lake Erie was out there under the moonscape ice covering it.

"The only thing lacking here is a kitchen," she told me. "If I had that, I'd never need to leave these rooms."

"Tram ought to be able to fetch you all you need on a tray."

Something flashed in Renee's eyes to tell me the remark had been inappropriate. She walked over to a side bar to pour whiskey in a glass that already had ice cubes and liquor in it. "Fix one for you?"

"No, thanks. What's your problem?"

Renee put half her drink away before she walked over to the French doors and looked out at the lake. "I was standing about here this morning when I saw it."

I looked out the window now and saw only the same bleak winter scene as before. "What?"

"Straight out from the dock." She pointed a forefinger with a long red nail. I sighted down it, across the dock out on to the broken ice that jutted up like scale models of mountain ranges. Finally I saw it too, a splash of color in all that gray. It fluttered, now in sight, now gone.

"Well?"

"Ice fishermen are on the lake all winter. It's probably a sweater or a blanket that blew away and got stuck in the ice."

"Bullshit."

I took no offense. I hadn't believed it either. "You want me to go out and see?"

"Maybe I don't want to know." She took another pull on her whiskey. "Maybe I'd better find out."

"You didn't have to call me. You could have sent Tram out there."

"He wasn't here when I arrived last night. I had to do everything myself."

I looked out across the bleak arctic landscape one more time. "I don't know. Why should I risk frostbite? If you want it checked out, call Bremmel. He has some muscle men to do the heavy work."

"I can't." Her eyes had an appeal in them. "I owe too much to them already. You keep promising to help me. Well, here's your chance."

So there I was, trapped by my own promise. I studied the snow-covered lawn. Even from this high angle I could make out no sign of footprints, but the way the wind was swirling snow around, that might not have been significant. "I'm not dressed for it. Did your husband keep any heavy coats in the house?"

For an answer, she showed me the way to the walk-in closet off the master bedroom—two of them really, his and hers. Lassiter had a rack of suits there that would have stocked a corner of Brooks Brothers, along with shoes and shirts laid out in plastic trays, but no outerwear. Downstairs in the hall closet I found his topcoats, tailored to match his suits, and also a camel-hair duffel coat with a hood hanging down its back like a knapsack. I put that on over my topcoat, Lassiter having been enough larger than me to allow it. I flipped the hood over my head and tied a wool scarf over my lower face as if I were getting ready to stick up a stagecoach. At least I had had the foresight to wear heavy hiking boots with soles like the treads of tractor tires.

Fortified against the elements, I exited the house by a back door and trudged across the lawn toward the dock. The instant the wind hit me, I felt naked. Obviously my time spent in milder climes had spoiled me for Ohio winters. At the end of the dock, I jumped down onto the frozen lake and continued my journey, glancing back to shore every few steps to keep my bearings. With the wind blowing snow in my face, it would have been all too easy for a city boy to get confused and wander aimlessly on the ice without any sense of where the shore was.

Every winter on Lake Erie brings news stories of ice fishermen who find themselves afloat on ice floes and need to be rescued by the Coast Guard. Those incidents occur later, toward spring, when the melting starts. Lake Erie, the shallowest of the Great Lakes, normally freezes over by Christmas, shutting down shipping until sometime past Easter. Now in late January, this close to shore, I had no worries about breaking through the ice. I climbed up a mini-mountain range six feet high, took another bearing on the shore, descended into the valley, and climbed to the spine of the next range.

He was half buried in snow, wearing a mackinaw with a wool scarf around his throat and a wool cap on his head. The long end of the plaid scarf blowing free had been the object we had seen fluttering. He was lying on his side, exposing the back of his head to me, letting me see the entrance wound behind his left ear. It was getting to be a standard M.O.

Tram had come a long way from the rice paddies of Vietnam to die here. I thought about the bad joke I had made to Helen about Tram being a criminal mastermind. I thought about the gun with two shots fired that had been in the glove box of Homer Tracey's pickup truck. I wondered if I now had accounted for the second one.

I trudged back up to the house and shed my coats downstairs. Upstairs I found Renee smoking and pouring another drink.

"Well?" she asked.

"It's Tram, the houseboy."

"I wondered where he had gone, why he wasn't around." She doused her cigarette and downed her liquor. "Why would he wander out there?"

"Someone made him, holding a gun on him. They made him get down on his knees and then shot him in the back of the head."

"Oh God!" The glass slipped out of her fingers, hitting the carpet without breaking, spilling ice cubes and liquor. She didn't notice it. "No more! Please!"

I wasn't sure whom she was addressing—God or me or someone else. My mind was on another problem. Three people had been murdered, all of them connected with this house—owner, chauffeur, houseboy. I was missing something that linked them, something contained within the walls here.

"What are you going to do?" Renee asked.

"Call the police."

"No!" Two steps brought her close enough to clutch my arm. "Don't do it. I can't take any more of this, don't you see? I can't handle it!"

"I have to. The police will need this for their monthly report. It's important for them to have an accurate count of the number of stiffs in their jurisdiction."

"No."

"Yes it is. If they lose count, the entire fabric of society starts falling apart."

"They'll think I did it."

"Not necessarily. Tram was killed while you were in Las Vegas." But I didn't say it with feeling. The refrigerator conditions on the lake would have upset all the timetables. "Did you kill him?"

"Of course not." Her grip on my forearm was not strong enough to be painful but the pressure was there, tightening noticeably.

"People keep dying around you, Renee. I really don't care if you're doing it. You're causing it because you're playing games with Bremmel or Lagrasso."

"Not out of choice. You believe that, don't you?" Her eyes were six feet from mine, probing me.

"I believe they've got a hold on you. I believe the best way for you to break that hold is to tell me about it."

"I don't want to talk about it. I don't want you to call the police." Her grip relaxed on my arm and slid up my bicep to my shoulder, then around the back of my neck. Her other arm joined it. "I want to go to bed with you." She moved her face closer to mine, letting her long lashes fall on her cheeks, letting her lips brush mine oh-so-gently. "I've wanted you to fuck me from the minute I first saw you." She kissed a little more firmly. "I wanted you when I saw your body in your swimming trunks. You want to fuck me, too. I saw it in your eyes." She kissed again, this time with her mouth open, her tongue darting, her pelvis rubbing against me.

Disentangling her arms from my neck was not the easiest thing I had ever done. "It won't work. You're going to have to tell me what they have on you."

She backed away from me, shaking her head, eyes wide in fear. "I can't. It's too awful."

I could have argued with her further about it. Better yet, I could have let her take me to her bed to seal our confidences. I could have tried a lot of things to get it out of her, but the expression in her eyes was enough to scotch all those plans. She was afraid of what they could do to her, maybe more afraid of them than of a chair wired to fifty thousand volts.

I called the police and asked for Captain Riordan.

20

Riordan was on duty that day in full uniform, including what the Mounties call a muskrat hat with fur earflaps that snap together atop the skull, the one article of clothing that can make any man look idiotic. Perched above Riordan's pouch-filled face, it looked good. Not that he needed it. He stayed close to the house while the lower echelons got cold looking at Tram's body. Maybe because he never saw the body up close, Riordan didn't seem overly enthusiastic about finding the killer.

None of that made me any less cautious about some of the deceptions I would have to pull on him.

"Last time I saw the little guy alive was the night of Lassiter's murder, week ago tomorrow," Riordan said while supervising the investigation from Renee's sitting room window. "Either of you seen him since?"

Renee and I mumbled that we hadn't. She said, "The last time I saw him was a few minutes before I left here with Mr. Disbro that night."

"And I tried talking to him after the two of you left, not that it did me any good," Riordan added. "I think the little bastard was lying to me."

"Why's that?" I asked.

"He knew more about Lassiter's murder than he would say. Maybe he saw Gruznik do the job and tried to blackmail him, so Gruznik snuck back and wasted him. Big-shot detective like you ought to know the second murder is always a result of the first. Don't you read any paperbacks?"

"I stick with serious stuff, like Hardy."

"Stan Laurel's partner?"

"The other one, the one who died a while back. How did you come up with this brilliant insight?"

"Simple logic," Riordan pointed out. "We've had an all-points out on Lassiter's Mercedes, not exactly the kind of car that you lose in a parking lot. Nothing has come in. That means the Mercedes is out of sight, in a garage, tucked away. It also means Gruznik didn't go far. If he didn't go far, he's still in the area. Which makes it easy for him to double back and kill Tram."

I almost wished I could point out his errors, but that was a pleasure I would have to forgo if I kept failing to report dead bodies.

"Plus," Riordan added, "we know that Gruznik is connected. By this time he has sold the Mercedes to a chop shop. Or it's been repainted and outfitted with phony plates and a new serial number."

"Doesn't it bother you," I asked, "that Lassiter was beaten to death and Tram was shot? If Gruznik has a gun, why didn't he use it on Lassiter?"

"Maybe he didn't have it when he killed Lassiter. Maybe he only got it later."

Click! Something that Riordan had just said meshed mental gears for me. But in some other context. What?

"It's plain we're not going to learn much here," Riordan was saying. "The wind long ago destroyed any tracks in the snow. If you folks hadn't spotted the body when you did, he would probably have been lying there until the ice melted. Then the currents could have carried him God knows where."

"So what will you do about Tram?"

"Can't do much until we find Gruznik. When we clear Lassiter's murder, we clear Tram's."

So much disappointment lay in his future I couldn't bring myself to hasten it on. Riordan had no further use for me, except to request a written statement, so I was dismissed. Renee took me downstairs to the front door, through the hallway where cops had wandered in to get out of the cold or sneak a smoke. At the front door, out of earshot of a soft voice, we had parting words.

"I meant what I told you upstairs," she said, keeping her hazel eyes on mine, letting me see the invitation was genuine. "I wasn't only trying to bribe you. You'll always be welcome here."

"Is that what you said to Tram the other night when you sat over there?" I nodded toward the church pew along the wall. "It might have been the last private conversation he ever had."

Renee gave me more of an honest answer than the question deserved. "I honestly don't remember what was said. We comforted each other over Boyd's death. I told him not to worry about his job."

"Nothing else? It could be important."

"He didn't say much of anything. He could be very hard to understand, impossible when he was emotionally upset."

"Gruznik didn't kill him," I told her. "He left here that night and drove two thousand miles in three days. He didn't have time to double back and kill Tram."

"Then—"

I shrugged and patted her cheek. "Someday I just might take you up on that offer—after you tell me what Lagrasso has on you."

This time her eyes slipped off mine, finding the toes of her shoes on the floor. "I want to, but I can't."

"Meaning you won't." I waited for a response but she kept her eyes pointed to the parquet. I gave up and walked back to my car.

The Shoreway was beginning to fill with rush-hour traffic when I got back on it, but it was outbound from the business district, going east in the lanes on the opposite side. For me, it didn't get bad until I had passed Municipal Stadium where cars were slip-sliding across the Main Avenue Bridge. Once across that, I exited to Ohio City and home.

Helen was already dressed for dinner out and ready for her role as Superbitch, which she sometimes plays better than she imagines. She would tell you our relationship precludes jealousy (those upwardly mobile words being hers) but she often resents my being called away by my work, doubly so when it involves a comely woman, particularly when Helen has seen her to good advantage in an aqua bikini.

"About time you got back. I was wondering if I'd been stood up. You hardly take me anywhere anymore. It's been simply hours since we left Las Vegas."

"I got tied up finding a dead body."

She paused, tightening an earring in place. "You're serious?"

"I'll tell you about it over dinner, the way the blood spattered and all. First I have to make a phone call. How about bringing me a cup of coffee?"

I made the call from the phone in the study, charging it to my business credit card. With the time differences, I figured I was catching Deputy Farlow Hudspeth after his return from lunch. Whatever the reason, he was in the mood to jaw a spell before we settled down to business.

"Something has been troubling my conscience," I told him when the greetings were completed.

"Warning Mrs. Lassiter to light out?"

"That wasn't my doing. Some big people in Las Vegas have a pipeline into your courts."

"Figures. What is it that's keeping you awake these nights, then?"

"The day I took Homer Tracey home, he had a handgun in the glove box of his pickup. I swiped it, considering he was drunk. When we got to his shack, I unloaded it and hid it on a shelf in his kitchen. He doesn't know I did it."

"So?" Hudspeth had no knowledge of any crime involving a gun. He was looking for arsenic.

"There's been a shooting on this end. The body was discovered today, but it happened sometime last week."

The *ping!* of a stream of tobacco juice hitting the cuspidor was audible on my end. "So?"

"When I unloaded Tracey's gun, it had two fired rounds in the chamber. I pitched them into his garbage with the four live ones."

At least he didn't say "So?" again. He said, "Hold on, son. The way you're putting these ideas side by side, you're saying Tracey done the killing on your end with his gun."

"It's possible."

"No it ain't. When did all this happen?"

"Lassiter was killed Tuesday night. His butler was shot on Wednesday or Thursday."

"So there you have it. I could believe it if you told me Tracey dropped outta sight a coupla days with nobody knowing, but the only way he coulda got to Cleveland and back that fast was by plane."

"Yep."

"You can't get on a plane with a gun. They got metal detectors and all that crap. Even us lawmen have trouble when we're flying on official business."

"There are ways around it."

"You and I know that but would Tracey? An old drunk like that?"

"He could probably figure out to mail it to himself ahead of time. Not by the U.S. mail. By one of the superfast express companies that guarantees overnight delivery."

"Shit." But he wasn't denying my idea. "Why would Tracey want to kill folks in Cleveland?"

"You said it—he's a befuddled drunk. But he really loved his wife. Somehow he gets it all jumbled up in his mind that it was Lassiter's fault his wife died. He flies to Cleveland and kills Lassiter by a blunt instrument on Tuesday. Within the next two days, he shoots the butler, probably because the butler saw Tracey leaving the scene."

Helen had come into the study with my coffee, which was

now getting cold. She had been listening to my reconstruction with an expression of appreciation on her face. About time she recognized my value as something other than a sex object.

Hudspeth was less appreciative. He ruminated long enough to shift his cud and favor me with another *ping!* before he said, "You've got a problem. First you say Tracey went to all the trouble to send himself the gun. Then you say he beat Lassiter to death. Why not shoot him?"

The answer to that question was the end product of the chain of thinking Riordan's offhand remark had set in motion. "Because the mail hadn't caught up with him yet," I said slowly with a John Houseman emphasis. "When he went after the butler Wednesday or Thursday, it had."

Silence. Finally, he said, "Jesus Christ. You might have something at that."

"Listen to me, Farlow. Count. I told you Tracey's gun had two shots fired. It only took one to kill the butler."

"What are you saying?"

"There might be another body around, in your bailiwick or mine, one that hasn't turned up yet. Check around all the places you can think of. See what you come up with." I said that much in the hope he would eventually think to check Winch's place in Stateline. It was as far as I dared go in telling him that Gruznik would be waiting there.

"I'll also check on Tracey," he promised. "What kind of gun am I looking for?"

"Stainless Ruger Security Six, .357, four-inch barrel with Pachmayr grips. He had it loaded with round-nosed .38 Specials."

Hudspeth had me describe in detail where I had hidden the revolver and where I had disposed of the bullets. "You'll find them," I assured him. "You're good at quasi-legal searches. When you test-fire the gun, you might want to send a sample to Captain Matthew Riordan of the Bratenahl police." I gave him the phone number and address. Before I hung up, I also got his promise to call me collect at my office number with any information he developed. I warned him Gladys would pitch a bitch about accepting charges but to ignore her.

When I had hung up, Helen was ready with a compliment. "In your better moments you can sound like Ellery Queen."

"But I was doing Philo Vance," I protested.

We ate at Sammy's in the Flats, where Helen insisted I explain everything I had been doing while she had been in her trance at the gaming tables. The exercise was good for me, requiring me to recap everything that had gone on. It retarded my digestion, but I got all my ideas aligned. It also let me see what I had missed.

I excused myself to go to the men's room, but I was really after the pay phone. I called the Bond Court Hotel to ask if Mr. Winch had checked in yet. The desk clerk assured me he had and offered to connect me with his room.

"Never mind. I won't disturb him this late."

"Very well."

"By the way, he was expecting a very important package. Would you know if it has arrived yet?"

"Several hours ago," he told me. "I sent it up to his room with the bellhop."

21

My appointment with Fox Fax was for eleven o'clock the next morning. Gladys had set it up for me, making it sound professional like two doctors conferring on the best treatment for the patient. With a quarter hour to spare, I drove out St. Clair past East Twenty-first Street. The snow had stopped, and an anemic sun was breaking through the clouds. I parked at a meter that had bent over at a crazy angle and flagrantly violated the law by crossing the street in the middle of the block to the building I wanted. It was a squat three-story brick with a restaurant supply warehouse taking up half its ground floor while the other half was boarded up with plywood slabs.

I entered between the two parts and climbed creaking stairs to the second floor. Half the offices were empty, probably the reason that Fox Fax had space on both sides of the hall. The inside part had a solid steel door labeled DARKROOM and was little more than a converted closet. A red bulb over the door showed when the room was in use. It was out. The other side of the hall, with windows looking down on St. Clair, was the executive suite. I entered that one.

The outer office was a cramped waiting room with space for two chairs in diagonally opposite corners. A magazine rack nailed to the wainscoting held aging copies of *Reader's Digest, Cosmopolitan, Ebony,* and *Newsweek.* I crossed the linoleum floor and looked through the main office door, which was ajar. The office was sparsely furnished with only the bare necessities for business, dominated by a chipped wooden desk. At the desk was the only splash of color in the place.

"Hey, Gil, baby." Gus Fox was a balding man in his forties whose ideal of sartorial splendor was a racetrack tout. Looking directly at his plaid sports coat was like staring at the flame of an acetylene torch. His pinkish double-knit checked pants, his yellow shirt, and his purple tie barely clashed with his beige plastic shoes and orange socks. He removed his feet from his desk in my honor and came around it to shake hands. "How's it hangin' these days, Gil?"

"Not bad."

Standing, he was half a head shorter than I am, his rotund belly pushing out over his trousers. When he moved, his sports coat peeled back to reveal gaudy red suspenders.

"God almighty, it was good to hear when your girl called today. You still bounty hunting for Moe Glickman?"

"Off and on." I forced myself to dwell on the fact that Gus Fox was working to be affable. His efforts to be friendly couldn't help coming out smarmy and patronizing. Even when he was trying to prove we were comrades, his eyes were sliding to all points in the room as he calculated how he could take advantage of our transient friendship.

"When you going to pull out of there and set up your own agency?" he asked.

"No hurry. Business isn't that good and Moe has been more than decent to me through some rough times."

Fox steered me to his client's chair and went behind his desk. "Any chance you're going to be called back to the police department?"

I shrugged. "I'm way down the seniority list if they ever start calling in the layoffs."

171

He nodded. "Know how it goes." Fox was back to his wooden swivel chair, slithering into it like a little boy who had sneaked into the principal's office and was trying out the seat. He tilted the chair back. "Say, what brings you here anyway? I been guessing ever since I got the phone call, and I think I've got it. Makes it easier on you if I say it, all right? Your wife went to work for that TV station, where she's getting humped by the weatherman. Common knowledge. Don't sweat it. We'll get the proof."

"No need," I told him. "Linda and I are history. Divorced. Final. Kaput."

He contradicted me with a shake of his head. "Never happens that way. Ex-wives, you think you're through with them, they keep turning up. It always helps to have an edge on them. We'll get you proof."

"It's not me, Gus. It's an old case of yours I wanted to discuss. It involved a couple named Carnahan where the wife was carrying on with a man named Boyd Lassiter. Sound familiar?"

Fox took off his rose-tinted aviator glasses and pinched his nose. "Carnahan. Oh Jesus, that one? Wife's a cute little thing, looks about sixteen, but she's a stockbroker? Fuckin'-A I remember that one! You picked yourself a dandy."

"In what way?"

"I'll show you." He put his glasses on to see while he riffled through index cards in his desk drawer. The index card told him what he needed, probably a case number, and he headed for the drawers of his file cabinet. "This one is filed under C—not for 'Carnahan.' For 'cunnilingus.'"

Fox pulled a file folder out of his drawer and sat down with it in his lap, out of my reach. "How come you want to see this?"

"She's involved in an investigation I'm working on. Maybe you've got something in there that would be of help." It was cold in Fox's office. I had not taken off my topcoat, yet I was feeling no discomfort. Either he sincerely believed in energy conservation, or he was scrimping on his heating bill.

Fox held back. "We might have an ethical problem here. I worked this case for the husband's lawyer. The idea wasn't to

172

gather evidence for the divorce. It was to get some really nasty stuff that would embarrass her so bad they could use it to jew down her support demands. The way it turned out, it never came up as evidence. The husband's lawyer showed it to her lawyer. That was all it took. The wife settled for a minimum out of court."

Ethics? He'd torn that page out of his dictionary. Keeping my face from breaking up, I took out my wallet and pulled out a twenty of Lassiter's money, surprised to see how much of it had disappeared during my western swing. I laid the twenty on Fox's scarred desk. "I expected to pay you for your time. You're saving me a lot of legwork."

Fox took the money. "Do you want dates and times and places? Or should we start with the nitty-gritty?"

"Let's go right to the pictures," I said.

He pulled an eight-by-ten glossy out of the folder. "This is my masterpiece. Look at the knockers on that broad. Them nipples must be an inch long."

His camera had caught Audrey Carnahan with her head tilted back, eyes closed, lips parted in ecstasy. There was also a man in the photo whose face was occupied with better things than looking at the camera. He was a back, a pair of hairy buttocks, and hairier legs that might have been identifiable in the right kind of lineup.

"Table-grade," Fox judged. "USDA prime. Shit, you'd go down on that in a minute."

"Got anything to show who the man is?"

He had a series of photos snapped within seconds of the master shot. Startled by the first pop of the strobe, Boyd Lassiter had pulled his face out of Audrey's muff and looked back over his shoulder to find the source. "Nice work," I said.

Fox fielded the professional compliment with becoming modesty. "That's why I'm known as the best in the business." By his own lights, he probably was.

"How long would it take to get a copy of this one?" I held up the master shot.

"Got a collection, huh?" Fox took a bottle out of a desk drawer along with two paper cups. "Still not using this stuff?"

"Still not."

Fox poured a measure into one of the cups, put his bottle and the unused cup away, and sipped some of his drink while he considered the effort it would take him to slide the negative into the enlarger, expose a sheet of paper, bathe it, and dry it. "Couple hours. If you don't want to wait, I could sell you that print for—oh—ten dollars?"

Besides the photo, my ten dollars bought me a brown manila envelope to transport it. Part of his ethical standards, I supposed. For one of the few times in my life, I regretted not accepting an offer of a drink. There was a bad taste in my mouth I wanted to get rid of. I lit a cigarette as soon as I left Fox Fax for my car and smoked two more on my short trip. I U-turned on St. Clair and followed it back across town to the parking lot behind my office on West Third.

"Message for you," Gladys informed me when I started past her cage. Rolf only hung out his tongue, panted, and slobbered on the floor. "Somebody called collect from Reno but he gave a phony name." She had to read it one syllable at a time off the message slip. "Far-low Hud-speth."

"Obviously a phony." I took the slip with me into my office and laid it on the desk atop the manila envelope holding Audrey Carnahan's immortal pose. Noon here would be roll call time for the start of the day shift in Reno, meaning Hudspeth must have made the call his first order of business for the day. I punched Hudspeth's number in the 702 area code into my phone.

"Nice going, Disbro," he told me as soon as the minimal preliminaries had been observed. "Your tip worked out. I just got off the phone with that Captain Riordan. He's anxious to see a sample bullet fired from Tracey's Ruger for comparison with the slug that killed that Vietnamese butler out your way."

"You got the gun then?"

"No problem. I went out to Tracey's shack and told him what I was looking for. He signed a 'Consent to Search' form and I found the piece right on the shelf where you said it would be. Surprised the hell out of him."

"He thought it would be in his glove box." I sipped coffee, still trying to rid myself of the taste.

"Nope. He thought his wife had it."

I clutched the receiver hard enough to break our connection. "Likely story."

"I tend to believe him," Hudspeth said, "if you want to put any store in my intuition. He was hung over bad, not in any condition to make up quick lies on the spot. Besides, you planted the gun in his house, if you want to put a less charitable interpretation on events."

"I only transferred it from the glove box in his pickup truck," I pointed out.

"It could easily have been planted in his glove box, too. Best we've got here is a case where the chain of evidence has some gaps." Let the record books show that Deputy Hudspeth was getting picky about the way evidence had been acquired.

I lit a cigarette and watched blue smoke rise in my office. "What is Tracey's story?"

"He bought the gun a few years ago, registered it, all the right things, and then handed it over to his wife. Far as he knows, she took it with her when she moved out, but it wasn't among her things at the Triangle K. He hasn't seen it, though, in six months to a year."

"Convenient."

"Anyway, I've got it now. I spend half my time firing test bullets. It's like being on the firing range. First for Riordan and now for the CHP."

There it was, a Hudspeth zinger. I rocked my swivel chair back until my head was nearly touching the ceiling slanting down behind me. "Chippies? The California Highway Patrol? Why them?"

"Another one of your hunches. You wanted us to check for any spare bodies lying around, so I got hold of the Chippies to check on Winch's place across the California line and, by God, they found one."

"Winch is dead?" I asked innocently.

"We haven't found his body yet, if he is. The one we found was a guy named Gruznik sitting in a Mercedes registered to Boyd Lassiter back in your bailiwick."

"That figures," I said. "He was Lassiter's chauffeur."

"Also the prime suspect in Lassiter's murder, according to what Riordan tells me. Funny thing is I don't recollect you mentioning that your client had cashed in, but then lots of things are going on that don't make much sense. A suspicious mind might wonder if you knew about Gruznik's body before you suggested looking around for one."

"See why citizens are so reluctant to help the police? I give you a good tip, one that really pays off, and right away you start accusing me."

"Something else I learned from Riordan. The Widow Lassiter is back at her home in Cleveland. I'm mailing him a copy of the warrant we have for her. It should catch up with her in the next couple days, if you don't warn her off again."

"That would be illegal," I said.

"Something you should bear in mind." He hung up on me.

I stayed in my office until I had finished my coffee and my cigarette. There would be time for me to get a lunch before I made my next call of the day. The people I wanted to see would not likely be stirring until afternoon.

22 By daylight, even the dim glow of the winter sun, the Carillon Club looked like a different place, its imperfections exposed like an aging star who could no longer stand close-ups or harsh lights. Flakes of peeling paint showed on the columns in front, and sections of the foundation had cracked. Parts of the lawn had weeds growing through the snow covering while in other places it had bare spots. A shutter on the second floor had slipped off one of its hinges.

I parked in front of the building and entered through the main door, which surprised me by being unlocked because the place wasn't open for lunch. As soon as I crossed the threshold, I understood why. A clean-up crew was busy inside. In the hallway leading to the dining room, a maid was busy running a vacuum cleaner, its noise covering any sound I made. Because the maid's back was to me, I was able to climb the stairs without being observed.

This time no Nordic guards blocked my path at the head of the stairs. I tried the door to the gambling casino, found it unlocked, and entered. There were no windows in the room, naturally, but there were dim lights built into the border around the ceiling, like night lights, that allowed me to thread my way among dice, roulette, and blackjack tables to the arch to the office. There I knocked. No answer.

Voices came to me from another room not too far away. I followed the sound down a side hall that led to a door standing open, spilling enough light to allow me to find my way without having to feel along the wall. It was a private game room, dominated by a poker table and the chairs that would fit around it. None of the chairs was occupied, but the voices still kept up. A few more steps showed me the room was L-shaped with more space around the corner. That part was a lounge where people not interested in playing or kibitzing could amuse themselves. There was a built-in bar in the far wall with a television set on one of the shelves behind it. The voices had been coming from the set where Rod Cameron and Forrest Tucker were having a falling out that seemed to involve Adrian Booth, who was trying to keep them apart.

Too late, I realized the implication of that type of programming. I further realized that if the set was on, someone must be watching it, someone who might bear resentment from our last meeting. Yet the room seemed empty.

"That you, Fred?" The voice might have come out of a speaker, for no one appeared to be in the room. Then he moved, and I saw he had been reclining on the couch that had its back to me. He propped himself up to look over the back. "Well I'll be damned." Clint Pettibone stood up to his full six four in one fluid motion. On the screen, Forrest swung at Rod, who blocked it and threw a punch that sent Forrest sprawling. Adrian screamed. I was tempted to join her.

"So we meet again" is all I said.

Clint wore his Western shirt and pants, cowboy boots, and string tie, no Stetson but his hogleg was riding on his right hip. "You're the one who thinks it's tough to kick a man in the balls." He started around the couch.

I glanced at the poker table, hoping someone had left a bottle sitting there I could grab by the neck, smash, and threaten him with its jagged edges. No such luck. Anyway only villains did things like that. "Didn't you learn your lesson the last time?"

"God must love me," Clint concluded. "He brought me all this way and delivered you into my hands."

He was clear of the couch now, taking the first of three steps that would bring us close enough to make me wonder if my mouthwash really was effective this late in the day. Rod and Forrest were duking it out, a foreshadowing of what was about to transpire in this room. I balanced myself, ready for it.

"This is about the most childish thing I ever saw."

The voice of common sense. I looked over my shoulder to see who was using it. Duane Lagrasso, of all people. He wore a blue-and-red-striped rugby shirt with a pair of stone-washed denim jeans. His hair was tousled, his face still unshaven. He carried a set of ledgers in one hand and a Styrofoam cup in the other.

"We have a personal score," Clint told him in words that might have come from the sound track of one of the movies he watched.

"Then settle it on your own time." Lagrasso set his ledgers on the poker table. "Go watch your movie. If this man gets out of line, you can throw him out."

A brief flash of displeasure crossed Clint's face, soon replaced by a look of anticipation. "He can't help getting out of line." Clint turned away and went back to the television set to await the inevitable defects of my character. I hoped he wouldn't pick up any pointers from Rod Cameron.

"Clint's right about you," Lagrasso said as he dropped into one of the chairs at the poker table.

"You might be needing him." I jerked my thumb at Clint. "You lost one of your strong-arm boys. I learned just yesterday that Al Gruznik was clipped."

"Heard the same thing." He sipped coffee from the Styrofoam cup. "Breakfast time for me," he noted.

"Why did you plant Gruznik on Lassiter's staff in the first place?"

"I didn't plant him. Al worked for me in the past but not since

179

he was sent over on an extortion charge. He needed a job when he got out of Lucasville a while back. Lassiter was looking for someone who would be a half driver, half bodyguard. They got together and there you are."

His answer had been glib, the mark of truth or a well-rehearsed lie. "Who put them together?"

"The guy who plays piano for me downstairs, Steve Stockman." Lagrasso popped open his Gestapo cigarette case and took one out. "He's tight with Lassiter's wife, and he knew Gruznik from Lucasville. What do you call that when you ask around among your friends for a job? Networking?"

"I didn't know Stockman had done hard time."

"Trafficking in drugs." Lagrasso lit his cigarette, inhaled smoke and coffee. "It wasn't much of a sentence. Six months and out on shock parole, which is an indication of the kind of clientele he had. Stockman had enrolled in college for a couple courses, and his group played gigs at frat house dances, whatever they have. It put him in touch with the right people, and he started supplying cocaine to a group of mostly faculty wives. They all went to bat for him by writing letters to the judge and signing petitions. You believe that? The judge accepting the word of a bunch of junkies?"

"Renee Lassiter was one of them?"

"One of his customers, not one of the ones who signed the petition. Who was it said, 'The law is an ass'? He had it right, whoever it was. The law comes down on people like me for running a gambling establishment, provided my protection goes sour, but nothing happens to the suckers who place the bets. Same with dope. Businessman who sells the stuff has everybody against him, but the users get the royal treatment. The whole world is ass-backward."

"The main reason I never wanted to be a narc," I said, slipping off my topcoat. "Why didn't Renee go to bat for Stockman?"

"She couldn't. How do you think Stockman was nailed in the first place? Renee was caught dirty by some cops in a traffic stop. It had a potential of causing a big scandal, so Lassiter used all his influence to cut a deal. If Renee rolled over on Stockman, she could walk, and no one would ask embarrassing questions about Stockman's customers."

Lassiter had told me a version of this same tale from his perspective, but Lagrasso's account was filling in more details for me. "Stockman knew about this?"

"If he didn't, he had six months of solitary thought to dope it out in his mind, figure what went wrong."

"Yet Renee went back to him for dope after his release."

"A junkie needs a supplier. A supplier needs a junkie. Who can figure people like that?"

"Stockman might have been a little peeved. He could have sprinkled arsenic on her coke."

Lagrasso smiled at what he thought must have been a joke until he saw the serious set of my face. "You serious? Is that what happened?"

I lit a cigarette of my own, letting him wonder. "You seem to know an awful lot of details that are supposed to be secret."

"The protection money I have to pay buys me some friends in the police."

"Is that the hold you have on Renee? It doesn't sound like it would be enough to make her drain off her fortune."

"Don't answer him." That voice came from Clint, whose total attention could not have been on the movie he was watching.

"Are you taking orders from the Lone Ranger now?" I asked Lagrasso.

"Sometimes he relays advice from higher up."

"Bremmel? Where is he now?"

"Resting. Taking a nap from jet lag."

Having seen Clint here, I was not surprised to learn that Bremmel was back in Cleveland. "Maybe you should wake him. I've got a piece of information that might interest him."

Lagrasso snuffed his cigarette in an ashtray built into the poker table, afterward exhaling his last puff of smoke. "Let's hear it. I'll see how important it is."

"It doesn't come free."

Lagrasso studied me a little longer. "Nothing does in this world. How much?"

"A trade. Information for information."

Lagrasso picked up a deck of cards and shuffled them. He cut and looked at the one he drew as if his instructions were written on it. He put down the cards and stood up. "Wait here. I'll be back."

I was alone with Clint for ten minutes. Time for six commercials and the animosity between Rod and Forrest to build. Roy Barcroft got involved in it, sent by Forrest to take Rod out, but Rod was too quick on the draw for him. After Rod had killed Roy Barcroft, Adrian Booth hugged him in reward—which made it justifiable homicide. I wondered what had ever happened to Adrian after Republic folded. Maybe I should write a letter to Richard Lamparsky to find out.

Bremmel walked in with Lagrasso, looking no worse for having been awakened from his sleep. If his eyes had been bloodshot, I wouldn't have been able to tell it through his thick glasses. Things must have looked all right from his side of the lenses. At least, he recognized me. "What do you want to tell us?"

"First I find out what you have on Renee. Deal?"

The word of a man like Bremmel was not my ideal of gilt-edged security, but it was the most the situation would allow. "Deal," he said.

"Well?"

"You guessed right. She killed someone."

"Who?"

"The name? I don't know offhand. I have it back in Las Vegas. Some kid. Little girl, I think."

"How did it happen?"

"Car. She was drunk and ran her down. Then she fled the scene."

"How long ago did this happen?"

"Three years." Bremmel was full of specific data. Probably he was making it up as he went along.

"Where did it happen?"

"In Berea, near Baldwin-Wallace."

"Berea just won an award. They've gone five years without a traffic fatality."

"Maybe it was across the line in another town," he said after a pause. "Maybe it was more than five years ago. What do you have?"

Calling him a liar at this point would probably have brought on a right roundhouse from Clint. In a way, I had found out what I wanted to know. "The Nevada warrant for Renee's arrest has been issued. It should arrive tomorrow. The cops will be picking her up then, so maybe you want to hustle her off to Miami or wherever you wanted to stash her."

Bremmel was unimpressed with the news. "We have lawyers already working on motions to fight the extradition."

"Your choice." I picked up my topcoat and went to the door. Bremmel made no effort to block my way, perhaps a sign that I had increased in his favor. Before I could exit, Lagrasso picked up his coffee cup.

"I'm going to the kitchen for some more. Bring you back one, Otis?"

"I prefer tea."

Lagrasso walked along with me, saying nothing as we passed his office door and went through the gaming room. I waited for him to bring up whatever was on his mind. When it didn't come, I said conversationally, "I met an old friend of yours in Nevada, Viola Kravitz."

"Viola? Sure, we go way back."

"You even knew a girl who died out there. Her name was Shana Tracey. I don't think I ever heard what her maiden name was."

"Fowler. Shana Fowler was the one she used most. How did it happen?"

"She got friendly with Renee, who offered her some coke. Shana took it and died. Arsenic."

We were on the stairs by this time. Lagrasso quick-stepped to get ahead of me, turned, and faced me from a step below, his face level with the knot in my tie. The cleaning staff had moved on to another part of the building, so there was no one to eavesdrop or drown out our conversation with a vacuum cleaner. "That was the point of your questions about Stockman. You think he tried to poison Renee and got Shana instead."

"It's one possibility. Will he be working tonight?"

"No. It's his day off."

"So I'll probably catch him at home." As I started around Lagrasso, he grasped my arm. I stopped a step below him now, looked at his hand on my arm, looked at his face.

Maybe my stare was not enough to intimidate him. I'll have to work on that. He said, "Be careful what you do."

"You, too? I thought Bremmel was your designated threatener." I brushed his hand away. "I'm already treading carefully on all this."

"When Bremmel's through with you, I'll still be there. Remember that." More than ever he looked like a banana republic dictator eager to turn his chief torturer loose on any rebel. The scariest thing about these guys was the way they could indulge in every cliché. They probably all had filled out applications for prison camp guard.

"I'll be sure to jot it down on my calendar," I promised.

He nodded, and I went out the front door into the winter chill.

23

Before I went on to my next stop, I killed some time in a coffee shop in the cluster of commercial buildings around the intersection of SOM Center Road and Interstate 90. I could probably have spent my time more productively, but driving into Cleveland would have been a waste of gasoline when it meant that I would have had to turn around again and drive out to the eastern suburbs. I had prepared myself for the wait by purchasing a thick paperback with a swastika on the cover. It was about a young American citizen of German descent—actually an OSS agent—who penetrated Germany with false papers during the Second World War and was assisted by the underground in getting an appointment to the *Abwehr*. He was about to learn the Reich was developing the atomic bomb.

Early winter twilight was settling over the land when I looked up from chapter five. I dog-eared the page and went out to my car, heading down Interstate 90 to I-271. That freeway runs north–south through the second tier of suburbs on Cleveland's east side, becoming a principal route for homewardbound commuters. East of the freeway lie the really exclusive exurbs like

Chagrin Falls, Pepper Pike, Hunting Valley—places noted for large estates with white board fences, where people actually ride horses after foxes while wearing red coats and black derbies, where Hollywood crews come to film movies set in Connecticut. Lining the freeway are high-rise condominiums where half yuppies can live in urban style in a rural setting.

The one I wanted turned out to be an X-shaped building at the Wilson Mills Road exit. I turned off from the jammed traffic and made my way to the high rise, backing into a space in the parking lot. In the lobby, I buzzed the apartment with no success, hardly a surprise considering traffic conditions between here and downtown Cleveland. I went back to my car to wait, doing irreparable damage to my eyesight by trying to read another chapter of my paperback in the fading light.

She arrived in a green Volvo, parked, and got out, carrying an attaché case in addition to her purse. Still, I almost missed her because she was bundled up in a hooded tweed coat. Before I got out of my car, I snatched the brown manila envelope off my seat. I caught up with her as she was about to enter the lobby.

"Audrey? See you a minute?"

She waited, uncertain until I stepped into the light, coming from the lamps beside the lobby door, to be recognized. "I thought you were out west."

"I came back. I could have stopped at your office today, but I didn't want to go through Wayne. I've come across something personal you should know about."

Audrey Carnahan glanced at the envelope in my hand. "Why don't you come up?"

Pausing to pick up her mail, she unlocked the security door to the lobby and led me to the elevator. Audrey spent the ride sorting her bills from the bulk mail, her eyes straying every few seconds to the envelope I held. When we reached her floor, the seventh, she gave me the key to unlock the door to her apartment. Inside, she took a few minutes getting her coat and mine in the closet. "Would you like a drink?"

"No, thanks."

"Does that mean you're on duty?"

"It means I don't drink."

Audrey went into her kitchen, dropping the bulk mail in a wastebasket on the way, leaving me alone in the living room. It was about two plants shy of turning into a greenhouse. They were everywhere, hanging in macramé slings, on wall brackets, in pots on stands that blocked access to her balcony, in window boxes. It was far too much. Even if you allow for my simplistic value system—houses are for people, gardens are for plants—she had overdone it here. Capi Mafiosi have been buried with less vegetation.

Audrey came out of the kitchen carrying not a drink but a sprinkling can and a spray bottle. "I have to take care of my babies," she explained as she went from plant to plant giving them a drink. "Half of these belong in my office, but I'm keeping them here until the remodeling is done." Occasionally she spotted something on one of the plants that she sprayed with the bottle.

I waited until she was done, lounging back on her couch with the manila envelope on the coffee table before me. Audrey had to return to the kitchen to refill her sprinkling can before she got all the way around. While she was gone, she left the spray bottle on the coffee table. I picked it up. It had once held Windex but now, I suspected, contained something else. She warned me when she returned, "Be careful with that. It's poison."

"Bug killer?"

"I get it at the garden store. They mix it up for me in a big jug. I pour it into the old Windex bottle for convenience. I suppose I should paint a skull and crossbones on it, or something. But then there are no kids here, so I've never been concerned about it."

"What kind of poison do they use?" I wondered idly.

"Arsenic." She finished her tour of the plants and carried both containers out to the kitchen. When she came back, she sat in a recliner across from me. "Duty done. Now I can listen to what you have to say."

I handed her the envelope. "That fell into my hands today."

She opened the envelope, looked briefly at the photo, and put it back. She looked up at me with wide eyes that had never seen anything like the stuff going on in the photo, had never known that kind of thing existed in the world. "Well?"

"I didn't think you'd want that photo floating around loose."

"Of course not." She got out a cigarette and lit it, blowing a stream of smoke at the ceiling. Back to her Joan Crawford mannerisms for business. "How much?"

I shook my head. "It's not that easy. I want to know a few things."

"You want me to write down my memoirs? Details of all Boyd's kinks?"

"I want to know how deeply you were involved in his attempt to murder his wife."

Her eyelashes blinked. Once, twice, three times. She didn't know whether to smile or get angry, causing her lips to set and reset themselves. "Are you—" She cut herself off, remembering you don't tell whackos they are insane. "What are you saying?"

"You visited Renee at the Triangle K. It was more than a social call. You delivered her a package, a supply of cocaine."

Audrey inhaled raggedly. "So what if I did? Are you going to arrest me for being a drug smuggler or a murderess?"

"Neither one. The police can do that, if they ever learn about it." I gave her a couple beats to absorb the implied threat. "Where did the coke come from?"

"Colombia, I suppose. Isn't that where it all originates?"

"Boyd gave it to you."

"No." She said it quickly and then amended it under my stare. "Not directly."

"What does that mean?"

"He gave me the money to buy it and sent me to the dealer."

"Who was that?"

"Someone he knew, a musician of some kind he called Steve. Boyd arranged for us to meet down by the shops under the Terminal Tower at noon. I handed over the money and Steve gave me the coke, like buying a pack of spearmint gum."

"Do you want me to believe someone of this generation doesn't know how to buy cocaine on her own?"

"As a matter of fact, I don't." Audrey put out her cigarette. "Give me a couple days, and I could come up with a source, but not right this moment. You wouldn't believe me if I told you I had never snorted or smoked a joint at a party, but as far as using it regularly, I've never sought out a connection."

"Then Boyd did?"

"He only knew this Steve through his wife. Renee was the one who had been buying it regularly."

"And that's the package you took to her?"

"Well, yes."

I didn't like the equivocation in her tone. "Was it or wasn't it?"

She stood up and went over to check a leaf in one of her plants. I waited for her qualification. "Actually, Boyd and I used a little of it that night. Why not? Renee would never miss it."

"What happened to the package after you got done with it?"

"Boyd kept it until I was ready to leave for the West Coast, about a week later." She turned away from the plant to face me. "You think that wasn't a nerveracking trip! Get on the plane here, get off in San Francisco, get on again, get off in Reno. All the time I was afraid a German shepherd would come up to my suitcase. By the time I handed the stuff over to Renee, I was ready for a nervous breakdown. I'm not used to that kind of underhanded work."

I summed it up for her. "So Lassiter had the cocaine in his hands for a week. We know nothing was wrong with it when you got it because you used it and nothing happened. That means Lassiter had to add the poison during the time he had it."

"He couldn't have done that."

I deliberately misconstrued her statement. "Didn't he have arsenic that you gave him?"

"That was for some plants of his own. He borrowed it because—" Audrey stopped, slowing herself down deliberately. "You're twisting things. You're trying to make it appear Boyd did something wrong. But that's crazy. It was Boyd who was killed. Renee is still alive."

"Another woman is dead, a woman Renee gave cocaine to. That was Lassiter's bad luck."

Audrey shook her head, coming back to the one fact she had decided would be her anchor. "Boyd was no killer."

"Maybe you're right," I conceded.

It was the most startling thing I could have said. She recovered from it slowly. "But—"

"Pinning a murder rap on a man already dead is too convenient. You bought the cocaine. The poison came from you. The cocaine was in your possession on a cross-country trip. You could have done it alone or you could have been Lassiter's willing helper. Which way was it?"

She put her fingertips against her temples and sank down again onto her chair. "A nightmare. This is a nightmare."

She was emotionally battered, vulnerable, helpless, the local cheerleader who had just lost her boyfriend to another girl. It would have been very easy to take her in my arms and comfort her. Instead, I stood up, looming over her, and shoved the manila envelope into her line of sight. "Tell me about it, Audrey. If you have any respect for Lassiter's memory, confess. Otherwise I use this."

"I didn't do it."

"Didn't take it to her? Didn't poison the coke?"

"I didn't poison it."

I grabbed a handful of her hair and pulled her head back so her face was turned up to me. Tears, of anger or of pain, were running down her cheeks, smearing mascara. "Please don't," she begged. "I'll do what you want. Anything."

"Tell the truth."

"I already have! You won't believe me!"

But I was starting to. "Confess that you tried to kill Renee."

"Fuck you!"

If this was a contest of wills, I was losing. "There are ways of finding out if you're telling the truth."

"Then find out. You'll see."

"All right." I let go of her hair, realizing I was not prepared to cross the line I was approaching. What good is a confession

190

obtained by torture? I could apply pressure but I could only go so far. So that's another of my failings. "I'll be holding on to this until I'm sure."

It was my exit line. I got my coat and left her sobbing in the chair, hearing her even after I was in the hall. I punched the elevator button, slipping on my topcoat, and when it came, I stepped aboard, leaned against the back wall, and lit a cigarette with trembling fingers. Before the door could close, a stout matron, leading a schnauzer and wearing the pelt of what might have been her last pet, got on. As the elevator plummeted toward earth, she sniffed and identified my Camel.

"Is that really necessary in here?" she asked.

"Lady, you have no idea how essential it is for me at this very moment."

24

From a pay phone at a nearby gas station, I made two calls. The first was to Renee Lassiter. I told her to pack for a couple days and explained about the warrant that would be served on her tomorrow if she stayed put. She agreed to be ready for me in a half hour, going along with orders as she had always done. The next call was to Helen, telling her we would have a houseguest in the spare bedroom. She was less cooperative than Renee. When I explained that this was business and an emergency at that, Helen came around, demanding nothing more than a full explanation written out in my own hemoglobin.

When I stopped at Buckingham Estates, Renee was ready with two packed bags that didn't seem quite heavy enough to hold the silver when I put them in the car. I started out the driveway with Renee beside me. "The reason I have to hide you," I explained, "is that Riordan saw you here yesterday. This morning he talked to Deputy Hudspeth out in Reno and found out there's an active warrant for you. When that warrant reaches Riordan, he won't have any choice but to arrest you."

Renee nodded as she absorbed that. "Where are you taking me?" she asked as if it really didn't concern her.

"Ohio City."

"How far is that?"

"Just across town." Amazing how some people can spend a lifetime in and near a big city without learning their way around.

Once more I took the Shoreway run to Helen's house, wondering if it wasn't about the tenth time I had driven this route on this one case. Not so unusual at that. The Shoreway is the primary east-west route of travel in Cleveland, and all my movement had been that way, including my jaunt to the far side of the Rockies. Those thoughts were something to occupy my mind until I reached home base.

Helen recognized Renee when I brought her in—the woman who had been poolside in Las Vegas wearing an aqua bikini. They regarded one another with the same gunslinger wariness as before. Finally Helen took her upstairs to show her the guest bedroom while I slapped together a ham sandwich in the kitchen. Helen returned in time to catch me eating it standing.

"You don't have to do that. I'll have a dinner to throw in the microwave in a few minutes."

"Give my share to Renee. I have to go out again."

"When will you be back?"

"Before prime time is over."

"Not very damned likely" was her guess.

Before I went out, I stopped at the downstairs closet and took out the shoulder holster rig that fits my Smith & Wesson Combat Magnum with a four-inch barrel. To balance out the weight of the gun, the offside strap of the shoulder holster holds two speed loaders and a pair of handcuffs. I strapped it on under my sports coat, over my sweater. I checked to make sure the Smith was loaded and went out to my car.

This time I almost got to my destination by coasting downhill without burning any gas. I passed the front of Steve Stockman's building, searching for an open parking space. I finally found one on a street angling steeply uphill, where I had to turn my wheels and set my parking brake before I got out. I slip-walked back through ice and snow to Stockman's building. Six people, three couples, were coming out laughing and shouting as I entered the mailbox alcove, Stockman not among them. I caught the security door before it could close and climbed up to his door. Even if I hadn't known the way, I would have been able to find it by the noise and the marijuana incense. The noise was rock music turned up to deafening proportions so loud it would cover my gunshots if I fired into the stereo, which I was seriously contemplating. I knocked on Stockman's door and got no answer, not surprisingly. I tried the knob, found it unlocked, and entered.

The apartment had the ambience of a crowded elevator with the Muzak gone amok. The woman who had been offended by my cigarette an hour ago should have been here. People were all over the place filling their bodies with mind-bending substances—drinking, smoking joints, tooting, inhaling crack. Finding Stockman in that mess was going to be a full night's work. Crowds, loud music, dope. Offhand, I couldn't dream of a worse combination. Every fiber in my body urged me to leave while my mind told me I had to finish what I had come for. I wedged my way through gyrating bodies not mindful of bruises I might inflict, searching for Stockman's face. It was nowhere in sight.

"Have some of these." A hand thrust itself into my face, the palm displaying a variety pack of different-colored pills.

Before I could slap it away, a woman wearing a backless lamé jumpsuit grabbed them and gulped them down. "Yummy," she said. "What are they?"

I didn't hear the answer in the din. I made for what looked like a clearing, but when I got there, I tripped over something on the floor, a couple locked in an embrace like the climax of a stag film. Two more lurches brought me to the stereo. Resisting the impulse to reach under my coat, I turned down the knob instead.

Silence.

The dancers went three more bars before they realized the music had stopped. They, as well as those who had not been dancing, looked toward the stereo to see what had gone wrong with their noise machine. They saw me standing there in a topcoat in an overheated room, one hand touching the stereo knob.

"What gives?" someone asked.

"Steve!" I called out in the silence.

"I'm Steve," said a short, chubby guy with glasses.

"Steve Stockman!"

"Over here" came the answer, near a hand in the air.

I turned the stereo on again, though not as loud as it had been, and made my way to Stockman's area. He was leaning against the wall inside a semicircle of mostly women, who were looking at him with admiration, probably either for his musical talent or his ability to supply dope. I broke through them and stepped close to Stockman to make myself heard over the music. "I've got to talk to you."

"So talk."

I moved even closer, squeezing his bony arm, and spoke into his ear. "Tomorrow the police are going to make an arrest. After that, they'll be looking to charge you as an accomplice to murder."

The words managed to penetrate his eardrums. I knew that when his head snapped my way. His lips formed "murder"? although I couldn't hear it. "Let's talk about it outside," I ordered.

I backtracked my path through the crowd, around the naked couple copulating on the floor, and felt relief when I was in the relative quiet of the hall. It was still many decibels too loud for the comfort of his neighbors. Already an incipient headache was thunking in my skull and tightening the muscles down the back of my neck. A moment later, Stockman emerged slipping on a John Marshall High School jacket. He followed me down the stairs, through the mailbox alcove and out on to the sidewalk without uttering a word. There he hunched his shoulders and jammed his hands into his pockets while his eyes checked out his neighborhood to make sure no one was within earshot. "What is this shit?" His words left a contrail in the cold air.

"Renee Lassiter had a bad batch of coke. She gave it to a friend and the friend died. Question: Where did Renee get it?"

Stockman's eyes showed he understood but he tried to brazen it out. "How would I know?"

"Cut the crap. You sold it to a woman named Audrey, who passed it on to Renee. If I found out that much, it's damned sure the cops can."

"God!"

"See what a neat fix you're in? Either they have you for an accomplice in the other woman's death, or they have you for attempting to kill Renee."

"Bullshit!" But it was only a word of bravado when he had nothing else.

"Tell that one to the cops. They already know Renee rolled over on you, causing you to do hard time. There's your motive for wanting to kill her. Tough luck the other woman snorted the coke first."

Stockman shook his blond head. "No way, man. I got no grudge against Renee. She was under a lot of pressure to do what she did. One thing I learned in prison is you can't let stuff like that eat at you. You gotta put it behind you, do your time, and come out on good behavior."

"Who taught you that? Al Gruznik?"

"That's right. He gave me plenty of good advice about doing my time. Don't mark the days off on a calendar. Forget the screws because they got nothing to do with running the prison. Stay away from the queers and take care of yourself with your hand. Lots of good advice."

A car coming down the hill from West Tenth Street went into a mild slide but came out of it in time to negotiate the curve. When we were sure nothing was coming, we crossed the street and walked under the rusty iron girders of the Detroit-Superior Bridge.

"Your forbearance is admirable," I told him. "How are you going to convince the police?"

"They'll have to believe me."

"Sure."

He stopped and turned to face me in earnestness. "Even if I had wanted to get back at Renee, I wouldn't do it by selling her bad stuff."

"Why not?"

He took offense. "My reputation. When it comes down to it, that's all that keeps me in business. I sell coke as pure as it can be found around here. I don't sell bad stuff. It's not worth it in the long run because it drives customers away. Go back up to my place and ask those people there. They'll tell you the same thing. Hell, ask Lassiter."

"Why him?"

"He came to me once and tried to strike up a conversation about ways you could mess with cocaine. Like how I could knock off a competitor. Just talking, you know. Always 'What if.' I didn't like it at all. I told him I wouldn't do that for any amount of money."

I started walking again, considering the story Stockman had just told me. Damned if I wasn't inclined to believe him. His stern code of business ethics was screwy enough to be true. "When was this?"

"Quite a while back, about the time his wife was leaving him. Just before, maybe. I should call him as a character witness."

"Lassiter is dead," I reminded him. "Al Gruznik killed him."

"Yeah, that's right. Poor Al."

We had been following a curve on Old River Road that swooped toward the river, near the historical marker noting the spot where Moses Cleaveland had landed to found this city nearly two centuries ago. That had been part of a deal with land speculators back in Connecticut. I wondered what Moses would have thought about this talk of dope deals in his namesake city.

Under a streetlight, I stopped and took out the manila envelope with the photo of Audrey. I showed it to Stockman. "Look at her. The face. Has she ever been one of your customers?"

Stockman looked at more than her face but I had expected that. When he had had time to get to her face, he said, "Yeah, I remember her. I was afraid she was a minor, she looked so young. In fact it was Lassiter who verified her for me. Say, is that his hairy asshole in the picture?"

I took the photo out of his hands and put it in the envelope. "When was this?"

"The same time Lassiter talked to me about bad coke. It was all part of the same conversation. He set the whole thing up for me to meet the quiff the next day downtown under the Terminal Tower, and we made the transaction."

"How many times has she been back?"

"Never."

We started walking back toward his condo. Triangulation, a term for map reading. When you want to establish a point, you locate it in relation to two other points—five hundred yards southwest of the hill at an angle of 210 degrees, three hundred yards southeast of the intersection at 120 degrees. You are at the point where the two lines cross. I had located Lassiter's position by a kind of triangulation. From Audrey and from Stockman I had fixed him as a man searching for the material to murder his wife. Arsenic from Audrey, cocaine from Stockman via Audrey. Maybe no court would buy it, but I was satisfied that my instinct about the way Shana Tracey had died, as I had told it to Renee by the pool, was correct.

"Am I really in as much trouble as you said?" Stockman asked as we approached his building again.

"Could be. It depends on Renee again. When I talked to her, she wouldn't squeal on you, but I can't apply pressure like the police."

Another car was coming down the hill. The driver of this one hit his brakes too hard, fishtailed, and went into a sideway skid. At the curve, he kept going straight until he hit a girder with his right rear fender. Instead of stopping and getting out, the driver spun his tires until he found traction and went on. Another unreported accident, or another stolen car.

"What should I do?" Stockman asked.

"Talk to a lawyer."

We crossed the street in time to see a black-and-white zone car pulling up in front of Stockman's condo. The two patrolmen got out, shoving their nightsticks into their belt rings and looking up at the light from Stockman's bay window. A second car arrived, and two more uniforms joined the first pair.

"My God! They're here already!" Stockman wasn't able to conceive that his loud party might have been the occasion for a complaint from his neighbors.

"I'd say you're about ten minutes away from arrest. Why

don't you find a bar down the street and have a couple beers? Slip the bartender something to tell the cops you've been there all night and had no idea what's been going on?"

Stockman caught on at last and took my advice by jogging off down Old River Road toward the cluster of watering holes beyond the Main Avenue Bridge. I went back to my car and drove to Center Street and across the bridge to the west bank of the Cuyahoga, then uphill on Washington to Ohio City. It was only nine-thirty when I walked into the house to find the girls hashing over my more notable character traits. Or maybe they were talking about Blake Carrington on *Dynasty*.

When I joined them, the conversation died. Within ten minutes, Renee was yawning, considering turning in early. "A drink before bedtime would be nice," she hinted.

"I don't think we have any liquor in the house," I told her. "I could run out and get something."

"Don't bother. I'll just turn in." With that, she went upstairs to the guest bedroom.

After she was gone, Helen moved closer to me on the couch. "Renee was telling me what you think about Lassiter's attempt to kill her. Do you really think that's what happened?"

"He made a pass at you. A man who would do that is capable of anything."

"Be serious."

"You met him. Do you think he would have been capable of murder?"

Helen spent nearly a minute in her mental jury room before she committed herself. "I think so. He was a totally self-centered man saddled with a wife who was an embarrassment to him. When he came into his sudden wealth, he couldn't stand the thought of seeing her get half of it in a divorce settlement. It would have been too much like rewarding her for years of misbehavior."

"Not bad," I judged.

"There was something at his core that was missing, a vacuum in his moral balance. Of course I know about the affair he was having with that woman student of his. When I was talking to

Renee before you came in, she knew almost nothing about her husband. He must have been living in his own shell without sharing their marriage. A lot like you, come to think of it."

"That's interesting."

"Do you still believe he wanted to kill Renee?"

"After tonight, I'm more certain than ever. I'm also certain there's more to it."

"Tell me."

"I don't know. Lassiter killed Shana Tracey by accident. Then Lassiter himself was murdered, then his butler, then his chauffeur. Why was that?"

Resting her head on my shoulder, clutching my arm, Helen thought it over. "They all lived in the same house."

"If that's a motive for murder, you and I are in trouble. What else?"

"They witnessed something that went on in the house."

"Such as?"

"I don't know. Do you?"

"Nope. Maybe I'll be able to work it out tomorrow."

Helen raised her head off my shoulder. "You do have something. What is it?"

"A notion that I can't prove."

She studied my face, which was supposed to have been set in a noncommittal expression. "Damn you, you're up to something. You do have a way to prove it, don't you?"

"Not tonight I don't."

"Tomorrow? What are you planning?"

"Me? I'm not devious enough to be planning anything."

"Not much you aren't! Now tell me: What are you going to do?"

"Think about it some more. I'll turn off the lights before I come up to bed."

25

Renee was the last to come down in the morning. Helen had an early lecture at the university, one of the Victorian era classes she had inherited, so she had first dibs on the bathroom. I followed her, making a hasty job of showering and shaving in order to get into clothes before I was caught undressed by our houseguest. When Renee did appear, Helen was about to go out the door.

"Behave yourself" was her last instruction to me.

While Renee got decent, I took my coffee into the study to begin the day's work. I checked in with Glickman's office, learning I was not needed. Next I called Audrey Carnahan at North Coast Investments and worked my way past Wayne to the boss. I told her to be in my office at ten-thirty to settle what we had talked about last night. I then called Duane Lagrasso to get a number for Otis T. Bremmel. When that was taken care of, I made one last call—to the Bond Court Hotel.

That completed my mischief for the morning.

Renee looked in on me, dressed in a charcoal-gray pants suit that, on a man, would have made her a banker. "What are the plans for today?" She was a good soldier, waiting for orders.

201

I wondered about her passivity again. "The main objective is keeping you out of sight when the police come with the warrant. If all goes well, I'll have that straightened out before the day's over. I suppose you'll just have to come along with me."

Our first stop was The Big Egg on Detroit where we dawdled over a late breakfast. The sun was out that day, a brittle winter morning that demanded sunglasses as a shield against the glare off the snow. We watched it through the restaurant window while we ate. I ate. Renee nibbled. It was eleven o'clock by the time I led her up the stairs to Glickman's office on West Third.

"You have a woman waiting to see you," Gladys told me. "I put her in your office." Rolf scolded me with a bark.

"Hell, that's right." I turned to Renee. "Mind waiting here? This will only take a minute."

Of course she would wait. She never had objections. Renee settled onto the bench beside a stout black woman clutching her savings account books, who was next to an unshaven man with a bandage around his head. I walked down the side hall to my office and opened the door. Audrey had been sitting in my client's chair, smoking and drinking a cup of coffee Gladys had fixed for her from my Mr. Coffee machine. She crushed out her cigarette and stood up.

"You're late," she accused.

"Sorry. It couldn't be helped." I poured myself a cup of coffee, set it on my desk, and hung up my topcoat. "I'm sure you'll think the wait was worthwhile." I took the manila envelope out and flopped it on my desk just beyond her reach.

Audrey's eyes were stuck on it. She raised them at last and looked at me. "You checked my story out?"

"As far as I could." I sat in my chair and sipped coffee. "It wasn't as perfect a job as I would have liked. On the other hand, I couldn't find any way to contradict you."

"Does that mean you're satisfied?"

"It means I don't have the heart to torture you any longer." I pushed the envelope across the desk toward her. "Check it out. You're welcome to use my wastebasket to burn it, if that's what you want."

She picked up the envelope and looked at the eight-by-ten. "I'll dispose of it my own way." She shoved the photo back into the envelope and stood up, looming over me. Once more the word "table-grade" flashed into my mind. "Saying 'thank you' is hardly appropriate in these circumstances."

"I guess not." I stood up and escorted Audrey out, down the corridor, and past the bench where Renee sat. Their eyes met, the way strangers' will, and held for an instant. They nodded to one another, and Audrey glanced back a second time, shaking her head and shrugging. I held the exit door for her, and Audrey Carnahan walked out of my life with a determined stride.

When she was gone I led Renee back to my office, settling her in the chair Audrey had just vacated. She declined my offer of coffee, but I topped off my own cup before I settled into my swivel chair and crossed my ankles on a corner of my desk.

"Did you happen to know the woman who just left?" I asked conversationally.

Renee shook her head. "A lovely young lady. Does she work for you?"

"She was Lassiter's mistress. Renee would have known that," I said. "Of course, Shana Tracey wouldn't."

I could have achieved the same effect by punching her in the stomach. She grunted, "Unnnh," and swallowed as if breakfast were trying to come up. "Shana?" She was fighting to control herself. "I don't think—I—understand."

"You understand all right. You're not Renee Lassiter. You're Shana Tracey."

"This is prepos——" It was too big a word for her to get out at once. "Preposterous!" She stood up and turned toward the door. "I don't have to stay here and take this."

"Oh, good. You're running away. I was afraid you were going to stay and deny it."

She stopped with her hand on the doorknob. I saw her shoulders square as she prepared to turn and face me. "Of course I deny it." Like a good actress, she began to assume an imperious air befitting a millionaire widow. "You don't have one bit of proof."

"Proof's easy," I said. "Police headquarters is right across the street. I have a couple friends there who would be glad to take your fingerprints. They might even give you a lie detector test while we're at it. If we go through all that, they'll insist on pressing fraud charges."

"Does that mean you wouldn't?" She was looking for a loophole for hope.

I shrugged. "I'm not your enemy. Let's hear about it."

She came back to her chair. "How long have you known?"

"A couple minutes. I've suspected it longer than that, almost from the starting gate. Lassiter told me his wife didn't smoke, but you do. So I began to wonder. Of course you could have picked up the habit recently, but when I gave you the chance to tell me that in Vegas beside the pool, you admitted you'd been doing it forever. There was also the way you drink. You can put it away pretty good but not with an alcoholic's compulsion. Last night when I told you there was no liquor in the house, you shrugged it off too easily. A drinker like Renee would have demanded I go out and get some. Added to all that, you've never taken any drugs or pills. That wasn't Renee's way either.

"These were all little things that add up and there were more of them. When I asked you at your house where Lassiter kept his overcoats, you sent me to the wrong closet. When I told you we were going to Ohio City, you thought it was a completely different town. Maybe Renee wouldn't know her way around all the back streets of her hometown, but she sure would know her way around her own house."

Shana was listening to all this attentively, as if she were genuinely concerned with finding out where she had gone wrong. Machinery was humming in her head.

"The big thing, the one point that really tipped me when I saw it in the right light, was all this jet-setting crap between here and Las Vegas, especially the day after Lassiter died. I thought it was Bremmel's doing, so he could keep you under his thumb, and maybe that was partly right. The real reason you got out of Cleveland so fast, without even waiting for Lassiter's funeral, is that you had to. You had to get two thousand miles away so no one who knew Renee could see you and blow your cover."

Shana had been recovering from her initial shock, adjusting to it as people will when they see the world falling apart.

"Winch told me a story about the two of you getting rid of a body, a story that was mostly true except for a small detail. The body was Renee's. She died after using the poisoned cocaine the way Lassiter had planned it. Somehow you and Winch ended up with her body on your hands."

"She hadn't been feeling well for some time," Shana said. "When she got feeling bad, she snorted coke. That only made her feel worse. Looking back on it now, I can see that it was the poison working on her."

I nodded. "Arsenic administered in small doses works that way. There's a buildup over a period of time until it finally kills."

"One night she came to my room at the Triangle K looking for help. She was really sick. I held her head while she threw up, and then I put her in my bed. Next thing I knew she was dead." Tears were sparkling in Shana's eyes. "I didn't hurt her. I didn't have any reason to. All I tried to do was help."

At least she wasn't denying it any longer. I sensed the truth was near. "You helped her by dumping her body in the desert."

"I was frantic. I called Harry for help, and the rest of it was his idea. I think it came to him the minute he stepped into my room and saw her dead in my bed. He thought it was me at first. Then he said what a shame she was the one who died because she was rich, and I'm not. And right then he thought we could switch places."

"Why not? You and Renee were close to the same size, so close you wore each other's clothes. You looked a little alike, in a general way, and Renee had one of those faces that don't photograph well. Winch's mind went right to work on it. You had Renee's identification, her checkbook, her credit cards. You could wear Renee's clothes and with the right makeup and hair dye, you could pull off a switch. The best part was that you didn't have to fool anyone who really knew her. Her husband, along with everyone else who knew her, was back here in Cleveland, halfway across the country. Winch must have figured you had at least a month of high living before the credit card receipts started coming in with the wrong signature. So you dressed Renee's body in your clothes and dumped her out in the sagebrush with your identification."

"Harry had the idea even then about going to Las Vegas to gamble," Shana explained. "Once I had established credit in Renee's name where no one knew her, I started plunging on the gambling tables. If I won, I kept the money, meaning I gave it to Harry. And if I lost, it didn't matter because the money wasn't mine. Harry kept betting against me, so one of us was always winning."

"Until Bremmel got suspicious." All this talk was making my throat dry. I sipped coffee to moisten my palate. "He wanted to verify your identity, and since he was coming to Cleveland on business, he came to Lassiter, who couldn't figure what was going on. He'd been waiting for word of his wife's death but instead of being in a funeral home, here she was gambling his money away. Something in Lassiter's attitude didn't sit right with Bremmel. He wanted definite identification—but not from Lassiter. Bremmel must have figured if you weren't Renee, you had to be Shana. Her body had been turned up by that time, and the news was full of it. Bremmel had one way of identifying you—by showing you to Lagrasso, who had been your pimp. That was the reason he had you fly to Cleveland and took you directly to the Carillon Club, so Lagrasso could eyeball you. He did, right in front of me, but he couldn't say anything at the time. He took you up to his office to settle things. Except I busted in to rescue you and take you back to Renee's home, only to find Lassiter dead."

I got up and walked to the coffee pot to pour a full cup. Sipping it, I told her, "That was your first hurdle. Tram knew you weren't Renee, but he was too worked up when we saw him to think about it. Besides, you were with me and he had no reason at first to think you were supposed to be Renee. Then, right after I found Lassiter's body, I went off and left you sitting on the bench downstairs with Tram. While I was down at the garage searching Gruznik's room, you had plenty of time to talk to Tram, to promise him money if he wouldn't betray you. Is that why you went upstairs to pack the furs and jewels? So you could hock them to pay off Tram?"

"Yes," she answered simply.

"And you hurried back to Vegas to find a pawnshop and get away from any friends here."

"Get away?" She liked the sound of those words. "There was no getting away. When Bremmel learned that Lassiter was dead, he took over. He put me on the plane to Vegas because he wanted to keep the masquerade going. Suddenly the stakes were a lot higher—control of Lassiter's company. As his widow, I would be in a position to swing things Bremmel's way."

"Pipe dreams," I judged. "He couldn't get away with it forever."

"Who needs forever? Bremmel was thinking in terms of six months, while the estate would be tied up in probate. With the right lawyers making the right moves, it could go even longer. He was considering sending me to Europe, where I could meet a plastic surgeon. Who knows how long he could have stretched it out?"

"Until," I added, "he had what he wanted, and the Widow Lassiter met with an accident, like a car crash in the Swiss Alps that would make her remains hard to identify."

She had thought about the same thing. Her eyes showed it. She lowered them and said softly, "I know, I know. Nightmares. But there was nothing I could do."

"Because Bremmel had you scared about the murder charges from Renee's death, which everyone thinks was your death. It could have been interesting if you had been arrested for murdering yourself." I finished my coffee and fished for a cigarette. "That was Bremmel's hold on you all along, knowing that you were an impostor."

She looked up at me then. "What happens now?" Shana had put herself in Winch's hands, then in Bremmel's, now she was doing it for me.

I wasn't sure I wanted the responsibility. "It's time for a board meeting to decide where we go from here." I stood up and reached for my coat. Getting into it, I touched the shoulder holster under my sports coat and gave it a little affectionate pat. So what if it was a theatrical thing to do? It made me feel a lot better considering what was coming next.

26

"Are you sure we should be going here?" Shana asked as I turned off Lakeshore Boulevard on to the drive to Buckingham Estates. "Won't the police be watching the house to serve their warrant as soon as I show up?"

"The warrant is invalid," I said. "It names Renee Lassiter, who's dead."

"Great. In order to save myself, I have to tell them who I really am."

"Would you rather go to prison?"

"I'm getting used to the life-styles of the rich and famous. It's hard to give up."

In the last half hour, she had quit playing her rich bitch role and gone back to her natural character, which was a whore. I'd been thinking that I liked her better for it. We rounded the last curve in the drive and passed under the arch into the courtyard, coming up on a pale blue Cadillac de Ville stopped there, its motor running, the tail pipe spewing white exhaust vapor into the crisp air. It was the same one I had followed from the airport a week ago. I stopped, got out, and walked up to the left side of it.

A smoked glass window in the back rolled down, seemingly

of its own volition. Otis T. Bremmel and Duane Lagrasso were inside, enjoying the benefits of the heater. The front seat was empty.

"See you made it on time," I told them.

"What the hell are you up to?" Bremmel asked.

Before I could answer, a staccato of pops rang out clearly on the brittle air, like firecrackers. I recognized the sound of small arms fire heard from a distance. "What's going on?"

"Someone else was here when we pulled up," Bremmel explained. "He started running away. Clint and Fred chased him into the woods."

"Goddamn those cowboys!" I hammered my fist on the Cadillac's window sill. "They're screwing things up!"

"All they're doing," Bremmel explained patiently as if I couldn't understand complex thoughts, "is chasing off a prowler."

"It was no prowler." I reined in my temper, resigned to the fact that getting mad would not change the situation. "Which way did they go?"

Bremmel pointed in the general direction of Lake Erie. "That way."

My first instinct was to go chasing off into the woods after the commandos. I had to put that off long enough to protect my rear. "Shana's waiting in my car with a key to the house. Let's go inside."

Behind his glasses, Bremmel's eyes blinked at my use of her real name, but he came willingly, not the kind of man who would bypass a chance to get indoors. Lagrasso paused only long enough to shut off the Cadillac's motor before he came along like a golden retriever. When Shana unlocked the door, they entered with me lagging behind. On the parquet of the hall, they turned to see me holding my Smith on the two men. Shana stood off to the side, out of this play.

"What is this?" Bremmel demanded.

I wish I could have come up with something original, but the best I could do was, "Reach for the sky, pards."

Lagrasso was slower to comply. He looked to Bremmel, whose hands were going up, before he lifted his own. Bremmel's eyes were on my muzzle.

"That's smart," I told them. "Now get over against the wall, just like on TV."

When they were leaning on the wall, I frisked them quickly. Bremmel's only weapon was a pocket calculator, but Lagrasso had a Centennial Model in his side pocket. Satisfied that they were disarmed, I herded them into the living room where I allowed Bremmel to sit on the couch out of deference to his age. I directed Lagrasso to sit on the floor beside him, his back against the front of the couch. Then I handcuffed Lagrasso's right wrist to Bremmel's left ankle.

That left them immobilized. For good measure I snatched off Bremmel's glasses. Now, even if he wanted to drag Lagrasso around, he wouldn't be able to see where he was going.

"Hey!" Bremmel protested.

I gave the glasses and the snub-nose to Shana. She held the revolver with a confidence that showed Tracey had trained her well. "If one of them tries to move, shoot him in the kneecap," I advised.

"My pleasure." Shana had a glint in her eye that appreciated the chance to dominate the two men who had been using her. She was so enthusiastic I hesitated to leave her here alone with them. Among other things, I worried that she would simply run away, unless she believed the promises I had made coming here that she would soon be relieved of her problems. I considered the alternatives and decided there was no other choice.

"Stay fifteen feet away from them, and you shouldn't have any trouble. I'm going to round up some strays." I went back out the front door to my car, stopping there long enough to get an extra set of handcuffs—my last pair—from my glove box. Following the azimuth Bremmel had indicated earlier, I slogged off into the woods, my feet sinking in snow deeper than the tops of my hiking boots. Sounds of gunshots helped me correct my course slightly, pointing me in the direction of the boathouse.

Moving from tree to tree to minimize my chances of being hit by a stray bullet, I made my way toward the nearest shots. I peeked around the corner of a tree trunk and saw a man crouched ahead, facing toward the boathouse on the lake. He was almost as thick as he was tall, holding a .45 automatic in his hand. Fred had purchased an overcoat since his first trip to Cleveland. As I watched, he aimed at the boathouse and fired, his .45 making a deep *boom!*

The response came much weaker from a corner of the boathouse, a puff of smoke and a light *pop!* that was almost lost in the wind. No wonder neighbors weren't complaining. We were isolated enough here that the sounds probably weren't carrying off Lassiter's property, a fact that struck me as having implications for Tram's murder. Off to my right was the sound of another shot, the sharp *crack!* of a Magnum that could have been Clint's hogleg.

The slide of Fred's .45 had locked open after his last shot, a sign that it was empty. Fred dropped the magazine from his pistol, searching his pockets for another. There would never be a better time to approach him. Five running steps closed the distance from my tree to his. He heard my feet crunching in the snow and turned at the last instant, gun in one hand and magazine in the other, showing surprise that I was atop him. Before he could do anything about it, I slammed the barrel of my Combat Magnum against the side of his face. He dropped the gun, he dropped the magazine, and he folded up into the snow.

I put my piece away temporarily and picked up the .45. I slammed the magazine into the butt, released the catch holding the slide, and put on the safety. I checked Fred, satisfied he was out of action for the near future. *Pop! Crack!* The remaining combatants were still banging away at one another. I crouched low, taking advantage of a depression in the ground, as I worked my way up behind the sound of the Magnum. At the bottom of the depression, my right foot broke through the ice over a small rivulet, soaking my foot and six inches of my pants leg. Drawing my revolver, I came out of the depression by another tree trunk. Ahead of me, Clint was standing behind his own tree, firing around it away from me, toward the boathouse. I braced my Combat Magnum in a two-hand hold, keeping myself concealed behind the tree trunk, and settled the target sights on Clint's back.

"Freeze! Drop it!"

How did I know he wouldn't do it? Maybe because Bill Elliot would have resisted, because Rod Cameron would not have given up, because Randolph Scott would have made a play. Clint spun and fired wildly at my general direction. The odds that he would hit me with that shot were slimmer than the chances in Vegas, but he wasn't really trying to kill me. He was hoping the shot would make me duck. Instead, I held my sights steady on him, now on the chest of his sheepskin coat instead of its back. Before I cranked off a shot, I moved the sights to his right shoulder and watched him pinwheel over backward. He wasn't faking. His gun had flown out of his hand, and I could see red spatterings on the snow beside him.

I approached him obliquely, keeping the muzzle of the piece on him. En route, I stopped to scoop up his Blackhawk and then came up close enough to see what damage I had done. Clint was alive. He bent one knee and groaned. The bullet had hit him in the right shoulder, leaving him stunned, unable to move effectively. Not many men can after taking a solid hit from a .357.

"Shit!" I said.

"Sorry—you didn't—kill me?" Clint asked between ragged breaths.

"I was aiming here." I poked my fingers into the center of his chest, six inches below his throat. It would build his character to think I had really been trying to kill him.

"Whatcha—get—for firing—double action." He swallowed. "Should've—cocked."

"I haven't spent enough time on the range lately." I frisked him quickly, finding nothing. "Stay put, for your sake if nothing else."

He moved his head in the ghost of a nod. I was gambling that his wound would keep him pinned to the ground as effectively as if he had a log across his chest. I stood up, half exposing myself. There were no more trees between this one and the boathouse. "Winch!" I yelled.

A pause. Then a voice. "Who's that?"

"Disbro. I took out both of them. It's safe to come out now."

"Prove it."

I stepped out into the open, keeping myself out of what I hoped was his range. He came out of the boathouse dressed in a bulky parka. I leveled my six-gun on him. "Drop it."

For a while I wondered if he would obey any better than Clint. At last he said, "It's empty anyway," and let his Walther clatter onto the dock.

"Up on shore," I ordered. "Down on your knees. Hands on your head."

When he was down like that—the same position in which he had put me when he had the drop in Las Vegas—I walked past him and picked up his automatic, adding it to the other weapons in my pockets. I came back to frisk him and then I got out my handcuffs and snicked them on his wrists behind his back.

"What's the idea?" he asked.

"There's two of them and one of you. They're hurting and you're not. I can't watch you all at once and I've only got the one pair of cuffs." I helped him onto his feet and marched him to the spot that could have been Clint's final resting place.

The initial shock of the impact had worn off Clint by this time, letting the pain sear through. He had maneuvered himself onto his knees one-handed and was trying to rise the rest of the way. A few more seconds would have allowed him time to reach a broken branch the size of a baseball bat. I clucked my tongue and threw the branch away, far out of his reach, before I pulled him onto his unsteady feet. Letting Clint set the staggering pace, I marched my two prisoners through the trees to Fred. He had come to and thrown up. Once on his feet, he was no steadier than Clint. Supporting each other, Winch following them, they wove their way up to the house. I pounded on the back door until Shana, .38 still in her hand, came to unlock it.

"Wounded man here," I announced. Fred led Clint into the kitchen and helped him into a chair at the butcher block table. I followed behind Winch and pushed him into a corner facing the wall. "Stay there."

Fred, his own face nicely purple from the barrel of my re-volver, began helping his partner out of his coats, gently sliding the sleeve off his injured shoulder and down his useless arm. Shana watched as each layer peeled off, seeing the blood soaked into the cloth. "See if you can help them," I told her as I lifted the Centennial from her fingers. Bremmel's glasses were in her coat pocket. I took them from her.

I took Winch with me down the hall into the living room where I had left Bremmel and Lagrasso shackled. They had not tried to move from the couch. Lagrasso's eyes followed Winch as I stationed him near the fireplace. Bremmel blinked off into space.

"What happened to Clint and Fred?" Lagrasso asked.

"They got damaged." I brought out my Safariland key and went to work on the handcuffs holding them. "I'm letting you go so you can help nurse them in the kitchen."

As the cuffs came off, Winch asked, "What about me?"

"In due time." I returned Bremmel's glasses to him so he and Lagrasso could head down the hall. I followed with Winch.

In the kitchen, now with Clint's shirt off, it was plain my bullet had caused a through-and-through wound, bleeding front and back. Shana searched around for bandages, coming up with some cloth napkins from the dining room. They made compresses for both sides and cut up a tablecloth to tie them in place.

While all this was going on, I stood by the kitchen counter watching Winch, whose handcuffs gave him no chance to pitch in. Lagrasso looked up from his work to see me lounging there. "Don't you have anything to do?"

"I'm into shooting them, not patching them up."

"He needs a doctor," Bremmel told me.

I looked at Lagrasso. "You know one not too scrupulous about reporting gunshot wounds?"

"Yes." He probably did, which conveniently made it possible for me not to do a lot of explaining to the authorities.

"Take them both."

Lagrasso led Clint out to the Cadillac, taking along Fred to have his head checked. When the three of them were gone, the number of cast members inside was considerably smaller—Bremmel, Shana, Winch, and me. I unlocked Winch's cuffs and took them all, my wet foot squishing, into the living room where I emptied my pockets of guns, unloaded them and laid them out on the mantel over the fireplace. I kept my own, still loaded minus one, in my shoulder holster.

Bremmel settled into a wing chair, Shana sat on a couch, and Winch stood behind her. I lit a cigarette and watched them.

"This is a screwed up mess," Bremmel opined. "I hope your purpose in getting us here was worth it."

He meant me. "I didn't expect you to try to kill Winch," I said.

"Bastards," Winch said. "I came here like you told me. The taxi dropped me off out front, but there was no one to let me in the house. Then this one pulls up and turns his goons loose on me."

"You ran," Bremmel told him.

"Damned right—when your goons jumped out of the car with guns in their hands."

I had slipped off my topcoat while the family squabble was going on. Winch still wore his parka, but Bremmel and Shana had left their coats in the kitchen.

"Why did you ask everyone here?" Shana wondered.

"For your sake," I told her. "The authorities in Nevada still have that warrant out. We should get that taken care of."

"I told you yesterday our lawyers would handle it," Bremmel reminded me.

"Not good enough. That strategy would be appropriate to Renee Lassiter, but this lady is Shana Tracey. I know it now, and you've known it much longer."

Bremmel took out one of his cigars. "If Shana tells the authorities that story, it will expose our scheme to milk Lassiter's estate. In that case, the deal is off."

"You're right. It is."

Bremmel turned his opaque glasses to Shana. "Look around you, dear. All this could be yours. Can you really adjust to the idea of being poor again?"

"It's not her choice," I said. "If she doesn't set the police right, I will."

Bremmel had removed the cellophane wrapper from his cigar.

He rolled it into a tiny ball between his thumb and forefinger and tossed it into an ashtray. "This could be worth your while if you keep quiet."

"The time for that is long past. It ended three killings back. Those killings are what we have to talk about."

Winch took off his parka and laid it over a chair back. He wore jeans and a turtleneck sweater under a flannel lumberjack's shirt. Bremmel said, "Those killings have nothing to do with our deal."

"Wrong. They have everything to do with it. Three people who lived in this house have died, all for the same reason. Lassiter, Tram, and Gruznik. What did they have in common?"

"Besides living here?" Bremmel shrugged. "Are you going to tell us the house is haunted?"

"Not in the way you're thinking, unless you want to count Renee's ghost. All three of them died because they knew her, because they could recognize her or at least recognize that Shana was not Renee. They died so they wouldn't expose the deception."

Bremmel looked directly at Shana. Winch, too, was looking down at the top of her head. It was Bremmel who spoke. "You killed them all?" He turned his attention to puffing his cigar alight, considering the proposition. At last he looked at me. "It can't be. We were watching Shana at the Caravan when Gruznik was killed. As for Lassiter, you, of all people in this world, should know how impossible that idea is. You had Shana and my people under observation when Lassiter died."

"Shana didn't do it. You didn't do it. He did." I looked up at Winch.

He tried a smile that refused to bloom. "Me? Why would I kill them?"

I tossed my cigarette butt into the fireplace. "You were riding the same gravy train. You could keep making money as long as Shana could keep passing herself off as Renee. Anything that would stop that was a threat to you. Remember what you told me about Shana's first trip to Cleveland? Bremmel sent for her, Fred got the airline tickets, and when he told Shana to get packed, she called you. You hopped an earlier flight and checked into the Bond Court because that was your prearranged meeting point."

"I also told you that I spent my whole time in my room waiting for her call," he reminded me. "I never heard from her until long after Lassiter was dead. If you're an alibi for Bremmel, you're also an alibi for me. You know Shana never had a chance to call me."

"It wasn't necessary for Shana to call you. You had a pretty good idea where she was going. You assumed Bremmel was taking her to Lassiter for the identification. That happened to be wrong, but you had to act on it before her plane landed at eight-thirty. You took a taxi to Lassiter's house, or somewhere near it, and knocked on the door. Luck was with you. He was there to let you in personally because he was waiting for word from me. You got inside, probably because you claimed to have information about his wife. Maybe you even suggested an impostor was spending his money and asked to see a picture of her. Whatever it was, you recognized an opportunity when you were alone with him. You understood that once Lassiter was dead, he could not expose Shana's identity. Also with Lassiter dead, Shana stood a chance of pulling off the deception to inherit his money. You grabbed the coal shovel from the fireplace and killed him with it, thinking Bremmel would soon bring Shana in to find the body."

"Wow! That's some story." Winch leaned over the couch to appeal to Shana. "What do you think of it?"

Shana looked up at him over her shoulder. "He's telling it like it is, isn't he?"

"You believe that?"

"Harry, I know when you're lying."

I lit another cigarette, letting them work it out while I wiggled my cold, wet toes inside my soaked shoes. When Winch stepped back, I went on, "The one thing you had wrong was Bremmel's intention. He didn't want to break up your little scam. He wanted to capitalize on it. Instead of taking her to Lassiter, he took her to Lagrasso. Then I came along and pulled off her rescue and took her home. Tram, the houseboy, had found Lassiter's body by that time. I left Shana alone with him a few minutes, long enough for her to cut a quick deal. Later that night, she made off with Renee's furs and jewels, with my help. As soon as she checked into her hotel, she called you at the Bond Court and explained the situation with Tram. You would have to hock the furs and jewels and give him the money to keep him quiet. Shana didn't know you had another plan for Tram. You killed him."

"I hear he was shot," Winch pointed out, "with a gun from Nevada. How do you think I brought that along on an airplane?"

"Tracey's gun, one he'd given to Shana. You found it among her things the night you left the Triangle K. I know that because it wasn't on her or in her car and Hudspeth didn't find it when he searched her room. You took it with you to Vegas, and before you left there, you mailed it to yourself in care of the Bond Court, not through the post office, through one of those guaranteed overnight express companies."

"You're not making sense. If I had a gun and if I wanted to kill Lassiter, why didn't I shoot him?"

"Because the mail hadn't caught up with you yet. It arrived the next day, in time for you to kill Tram. You came back here to see him, supposedly to pay him off for not blowing Shana's cover. Instead, you pulled Tracey's gun on him and marched him out on to the ice over the lake. You made him get down on his knees, and you shot him in the back of his head."

"The way those fucking slants did it in Nam. Nice touch."

Bremmel and Shana were watching Winch carefully. What he had just said skirted the edges of a confession. I took a satisfying drag on my cigarette. "With Tram dead, you had eliminated another problem. Now you got back to your hotel, packaged the gun, and mailed it back to yourself in Stateline, probably to your real estate office there. Then you caught a flight to Reno, picked up Tracey's gun, and went to your place in the mountains to use it one last time on Al Gruznik. Afterward you took it back to Reno and planted it in the glove box of Tracey's pickup. The way he was driving around, hitting the bars, he wouldn't have been hard to find. Or you could have found it parked at his shack."

"Wait." It was Bremmel speaking up. "Why was Winch killing Gruznik out there?"

"Maybe Winch will enlighten us." I waited for him to speak up, and when he didn't, I spoke to Bremmel. "I don't know exactly what happened between Winch and Gruznik. We know this much: Immediately after Lassiter's murder, Gruznik stole the household funds, got in Lassiter's Mercedes, and drove two thousand miles in three days—probably not a world's record but moving right along. He didn't have time for a lot of detours, so we have to assume he headed directly to Winch and got himself shot. It's a safe bet he had a specific destination in mind.

"Put all that together and you can make a reasonable guess how it went. Gruznik found Winch standing over Lassiter's body. Gruznik and Lassiter had had a falling out earlier in the day he died, so Gruznik had no particular hate for his boss's killer. Winch talked fast, maybe even giving Gruznik a rundown on the scam he was pulling with Shana. He promised Gruznik money—not here, of course. In Nevada. Gruznik helped himself to Lassiter's house money and Mercedes. He gave Winch a lift back to his hotel, then set out for Reno, moving fast that night because he knew the Mercedes would soon be on the hot list. How am I doing, Harry?"

"Nice story. As far as proof goes, you don't have dipshit."

The doorbell rang.

"Not much at the moment," I agreed. "Your best protection so far has been that the police don't know you exist. When I lay it out for them, they'll start digging for evidence. Before long, they'll have something to tie you into one of the three killings. That's all they need. You can only fry once. Before it's over, you'll cop out to all three to avoid the death penalty."

The doorbell rang again.

"Watch him," I told Bremmel as I headed for the hall. The caller turned out to be Captain Matthew Riordan in his muskrat hat with two uniforms, one of them female. He was not surprised to see me. He had a legal paper in his hand, foolscap folded into fourths, which he held up for me and started the official spiel. "I have here a warrant for the arrest of Renee Lassiter. Is she here?"

"No."

His already fallen face had nowhere to go. "I'm going to have to come in and see for myself."

"Sure. Do that. While you're here, I'll introduce you to Shana Tracey."

The name meant something to him. He looked at the Nevada warrant. "She's the one who—"

I cut him off with a nod. "Come in and we'll tell you all about it."

That meant I had to start the whole explanation over again. When it was done, Riordan was ready to arrest everyone in sight but settled for Winch. For the rest of the week I caught hell from him and from two other states.

Catching hell is part of my job description.